"YOU FEEL SO GOOD," HE GROANED. "I WANT YOU."

Reluctantly she moved out of his arms. "No, Jim, I really don't want to get involved this way. I'm very happy with my life the way it is. I have my patients, my friends and family—"

"And you're also a healthy young woman, so is that enough?" he interrupted.

Ashley glared at him. "Are *you* trying to psychoanalyze *me?*"

"No, I'm just trying to understand why you're afraid of getting involved with me."

"I'm not afraid. I'm just too busy for a romantic entanglement right now."

"Did I suggest a romantic entanglement?" he asked mockingly. "Maybe all I wanted was a one-night stand."

CANDLELIGHT ECSTASY ROMANCES®

266 WINNER TAKES ALL, *Cathie Linz*
267 A WINNING COMBINATION, *Lori Copeland*
268 A COMPROMISING PASSION, *Nell Kincaid*
269 TAKE MY HAND, *Anna Hudson*
270 HIGH STAKES, *Eleanor Woods*
271 SERENA'S MAGIC, *Heather Graham*
272 A DARING ALLIANCE, *Alison Tyler*
273 SCATTERED ROSES, *Jo Calloway*
274 WITH ALL MY HEART, *Emma Bennett*
275 JUST CALL MY NAME, *Dorothy Ann Bernard*
276 THE PERFECT AFFAIR, *Lynn Patrick*
277 ONE IN A MILLION, *Joan Grove*
278 HAPPILY EVER AFTER, *Barbara Andrews*
279 SINNER AND SAINT, *Prudence Martin*
280 RIVER RAPTURE, *Patricia Markham*
281 MATCH MADE IN HEAVEN, *Malissa Carroll*
282 TO REMEMBER LOVE, *Jo Calloway*
283 EVER A SONG, *Karen Whittenburg*
284 CASANOVA'S MASTER, *Anne Silverlock*
285 PASSIONATE ULTIMATUM, *Emma Bennett*
286 A PRIZE CATCH, *Anna Hudson*
287 LOVE NOT THE ENEMY, *Sara Jennings*
288 SUMMER FLING, *Natalie Stone*
289 AMBER PERSUASION, *Linda Vail*
290 BALANCE OF POWER, *Shirley Hart*
291 BEGINNER'S LUCK, *Alexis Hill Jordan*
292 LIVE TOGETHER AS STRANGERS, *Megan Lane*
293 AND ONE MAKES FIVE, *Kit Daley*
294 RAINBOW'S END, *Lori Copeland*
295 LOVE'S DAWNING, *Tate McKenna*
296 SOUTHERN COMFORT, *Carla Neggers*
297 FORGOTTEN DREAMS, *Eleanor Woods*
298 MY KIND OF LOVE, *Barbara Andrews*
299 SHENANDOAH SUMMER, *Samantha Hughes*
300 STAND STILL THE MOMENT, *Margaret Dobson*
301 NOT TOO PERFECT, *Candice Adams*
302 LAUGHTER'S WAY, *Paula Hamilton*
303 TOMORROW'S PROMISE, *Emily Elliott*
304 PULLING THE STRINGS, *Alison Tyler*
305 FIRE AND ICE, *Anna Hudson*

THRILL OF THE CHASE

Donna Kimel Vitek

A CANDLELIGHT ECSTASY ROMANCE®

Published by
Dell Publishing Co., Inc.
1 Dag Hammarskjold Plaza
New York, New York 10017

Copyright © 1985 by Donna Kimel Vitek

All rights reserved. No part of this book may be reproduced or transmitted in any form or by any means, electronic or mechanical, including photocopying, recording, or by any information storage and retrieval system, without the written permission of the Publisher, except where permitted by law.

Dell® TM 681510, Dell Publishing Co., Inc.

Candlelight Ecstasy Romance®, 1,203,540, is a registered trademark of Dell Publishing Co., Inc., New York, New York.

ISBN: 0-440-18662-5

Printed in the United States of America

First printing—February 1985

To Our Readers:

We have been delighted with your enthusiastic response to Candlelight Ecstasy Romances®, and we thank you for the interest you have shown in this exciting series.

In the upcoming months we will continue to present the distinctive, sensuous love stories you have come to expect only from Ecstasy. We look forward to bringing you many more books from your favorite authors and also the very finest work from new authors of contemporary romantic fiction.

As always, we are striving to present the unique, absorbing love stories that you enjoy most—books that are more than ordinary romance.

Your suggestions and comments are always welcome. Please write to us at the address below.

Sincerely,

The Editors
Candlelight Romances
1 Dag Hammarskjold Plaza
New York, New York 10017

CHAPTER ONE

There was a brief moment of heavy silence. Fred Naylor, Boulder, Colorado's, best-known local TV talk-show host, glanced back and forth at his guests, Ashley Miller and Jim Saxon, who sat opposite each other in the casual semicircle of comfortable cream-color chairs.

"Well, it's obvious you two disagree completely on this issue," Fred said with aplomb, quickly breaking the silence and fulfilling his responsibility to keep the show moving right along. He swiveled his chair slightly toward Jim. "Dr. Saxon, can you give us a few specific reasons why you're opposed to radio shows that encourage listeners to call in and discuss any problems they might have with a psychologist?"

"I can give you several specific reasons," Jim Saxon answered, his deep voice melodious and confident. "First and foremost, I don't believe in quick fixes. It's impossible for a psychologist to talk to a person for thirty seconds or so, then tell them how to solve all their problems. Given that little information, any advice offered would be haphazard, to say the least. Even dangerous, in some cases."

"If I may, Dr. Saxon," Ashley spoke up, her own voice firm and strong, with an attractive lilt in it: "I can assure you that I tell my listeners I can't possibly solve all their problems with quick answers, and most of them understand that. Most of the calls I receive are from people with minor, temporary problems, which I can usually help them with."

"You feel it's all right to give advice to someone without knowing about his or her background?"

"I always ask questions about background and extenuating circumstances. Anyone who calls me gets considerably more than thirty seconds of my time, Dr. Saxon," responded Ashley calmly. "But of course some problems are much simpler than others. Last night, for example, I took a call from a man who seemed to want me to agree that he had every right to refuse to allow his wife to go back to work. I think it was fairly safe to advise him to have a serious discussion with her about the situation. Surely you don't feel that was irresponsible and useless advice?"

"No, but I assume you're more than a 'Dear Abby' of the airwaves," Jim Saxon countered, his dark, intelligent eyes holding hers. "You must receive calls from people who have severe, deep-rooted problems that can't possibly be solved by a quick answer."

Ashley nodded. "When I do get calls like that, I don't offer quick answers or any definitive answer at all. I urge those callers to seek counseling. I certainly would never tell a severely depressed person to just snap out of it and get out and mix with other people. And of course I don't attempt to deal with psychoses or neuroses. The moment I begin to suspect a caller may be deeply disturbed, I do my best to convince her or him to seek help from a psychiatrist, such as yourself, Dr. Saxon."

"Well, this is interesting," Fred Naylor announced, his standard talk-show-host smile including both his guests even as he concentrated on Ashley. "I understand your broadcast is getting terrific ratings and that you get many more calls than you can deal with during your time on the air. Why do you think so many people are willing to pour out their problems when they know thousands of other people will be hearing them?"

"They'll be heard by thousands, yes, but they're still anonymous, simply voices with no names. I believe that's why many of them call me," Ashley explained. "Maybe they'd feel uncomfortable talking to a friend or relative about their problems. But they need someone who will listen, so they call me. That's perfectly natural. As a psychiatrist, Dr. Saxon knows that everyone needs somebody who'll listen."

Nodding, Fred turned back to Jim. "How would you respond to that, Dr. Saxon?"

"Listening is one thing; giving advice based on a brief phone conversation is another. There are some obvious dangers. For instance, Ashley," Jim said, using her first name as easily as if they'd known each other for years, "people tend to tell only their own side of the story when they're having relationship problems. If you hear only that one side and give advice, callers can go to their husbands, wives, whatever and say: 'I'm right and you're wrong. I know because that psychologist on the radio agreed with me.' That's going to cause more harm than good. And how can you be sure you're getting the whole story from anyone?"

"I can't be positively sure, any more than you can be sure you're getting the complete truth from your patients. But I can be fairly certain most of the time because I am a qualified psychologist and I was trained to ask questions that will usually bring the facts out. As you were . . . Jim."

While Fred Naylor again referred to the popularity of Ashley's call-in radio show, Jim regarded her intently, his chin resting on long fingers. He had expected her to be older, but his guess was that she was about twenty-five or twenty-six, and she was attractive in a very natural way. Not beautiful but intriguing. There was nothing flashy about her. Her navy blue suit was tailored, but the jabot of fine lace at the neck of her blouse provided just the right subdued touch of femininity. Average height. Slender but shapely build. Great legs. And she seemed relaxed and self-assured. He liked that. He'd always liked formidable opponents. His gaze wandered over her. In the studio lights, her short, soft blond hair shimmered like spun gold and her aquamarine eyes took on the clarity of a tropical sea. As she turned them toward him, he gave her a slow smile, then focused his undivided attention on his host, who was speaking to him again.

"You have to admit that shows like Miss . . . er, Dr. Miller's are popular, Dr. Saxon," Naylor said. "Although you and a number of your associates don't approve of them, it's obvious a great many people do."

"Which bothers me to some extent," replied Jim. "I wonder if such shows are becoming more a new form of entertainment than a service to the community. How many people tune in just to be titillated by other people's secrets?"

Ashley leaned forward in her chair. "I can answer that by simply saying it's very natural for people to be interested in someone else's problems. But I believe that's good. The more they learn about the human experience, the more prepared they'll be to deal with some of their own problems. Ignorance isn't really bliss, Dr. Sax —Jim. It's simply ignorance."

"On that point I agree. But let me ask you this. How many of the calls you take do you think are legitimate?"

"I can only guess, but I'd say eighty to ninety percent."

"But you're not sure more of them are phony?"

"I'm pretty sure. I can usually tell a hoax. Something in the voice just doesn't ring true. It's easy to deal with that."

"And how do you deal with the caller who chooses to share his sexual fantasies with all of Boulder and the surrounding area?"

"We disconnect," Ashley told him matter-of-factly. "But we don't get many calls like that."

"But you do get calls about sexual problems?"

"A few, and I try to deal with them. But I've told my listeners many times that I really don't have that much experience in sexual matters."

Jim quirked one eyebrow. "Oh?"

"Sexual problems. I'm not a sex therapist, Jim," she said, looking him straight in the eye, ignoring that innuendo. "In my practice I deal mostly with family counseling and group therapy sessions. And on my call-in show I hear mainly from people who are having family, social or career problems. I'm sort of what you might call a general practitioner of psychology, not a specialist, as sex therapists usually are."

"Well, that is interesting," Fred Naylor announced once again. "Now, Dr. Saxon, you said you could give us several reasons you opposed call-in 'advice' shows. You've mentioned a few. Any others?"

"Yes. For one, I have to wonder if the psychologists who host these shows and advise their callers to seek professional help are seeing a sharp increase in their number of patients."

Ashley's hands, folded in her lap, squeezed together tightly. She stared at him. Although she had felt surprisingly calm throughout this discussion, this last remark of his raised her hackles. Her neck burned hotly, yet she managed to keep her features composed as she said frostily, "I've never once advised a caller to make an appointment with me. I'm in practice with my father, and we haven't seen an abnormal increase in new patients in the six months I've been on the air. So if you psychiatrists, Dr. Saxon, are worried about us taking away some of your patients, you shouldn't be."

"Well . . . hmmm, we have only a couple of minutes left," Fred Naylor announced. "Dr. Saxon, is there anything else you'd like to say?"

"Yes. I have to admit I'm a little concerned that these radio call-in shows are nothing more than another form of pop psychology, entertaining but relatively useless. And I wonder if the hosts and hostesses aren't more interested in becoming celebrities than they are in helping people solve their problems."

At that Ashley had to laugh aloud. "I hardly think being on the air one hour three nights a week on a local radio station is going to make a celebrity out of me. I certainly don't expect to be named to *Who's Who* anytime soon."

"Some of your colleagues might be, though," Jim Saxon said flatly. "A few of them host shows that are syndicated and heard all over the country."

"I'm not 'some of my colleagues.' I'm not syndicated and certainly not a celebrity, so don't lump me in with them," Ashley retorted. "I expect to be evaluated on my own merits. Can you do that, Dr. Saxon? Have you ever even listened to my show?"

"As a matter of fact, I haven't."

"Then do. I think you should before you take it upon yourself to criticize me again."

Jim inclined his head, a half smile playing over his mouth. "I'll certainly keep your advice in mind, Ashley."

"Well now, this has been interesting but I'm afraid we're all out of time," Fred Naylor pronounced with something like a sigh of relief as he bestowed practiced smiles on both his guests. "We're delighted the two of you could join us today. Thank you."

"Thank you," Ashley and Jim murmured simultaneously.

As the studio lights dimmed, Ashley took her first really deep breath in nearly half an hour. She hated appearing on TV, especially live. Although she had forced herself to withstand the ordeal several times in the past six months and had learned to at least fake composure, she had never gotten over being extremely uncomfortable. Realizing she was in the camera's eye terrified her; seeing herself in the monitor always made her want to cringe. Only sheer willpower enabled her to fake her way through, and as soon as Fred Naylor stood, she did, too, said good-bye, shook his hand and exited the set as quickly as she could without being obvious about it.

After getting her purse from the women's lounge, Ashley stopped in the hallway to speak to Fred Naylor's director. After thanking him for having her on the show, she walked to the elevator, where Jim Saxon was just pushing the down button. When he turned and gave her an easy smile, she returned it. He was a handsome man, not male-model perfect, but there was strength in his finely hewn features and dark brown eyes. About six feet tall, he was trim and looked athletic although by no means muscle-bound. In his early thirties, he had sandy blond hair with just a touch of curl to it that somehow helped soften the perceptive light in his eyes. Ashley stepped up beside him, and when the elevator doors swept open, they walked in together.

"I enjoyed our little debate, Ashley," Jim said, watching as she pushed the lobby button. "You made some good points."

Tucking her leather clutch purse beneath her arm, she met his gaze directly. "But I didn't change your mind?"

"No, you didn't," he admitted. "But maybe you didn't have enough time. If you haven't had dinner, why don't we have it together so we can go on discussing our difference of opinion."

Ashley smiled but declined. "Thanks but I don't think . . ."

"There's a fine restaurant right across the street," he persisted, a mildly provocative note in his voice as he added, "and surely there's a lot you'd like to say that you didn't have a chance to tell me while we were on the air."

"True," said Ashley, preceding him out of the elevator when it stopped at the lobby. "But I think it might just be better for you to tune in my radio program sometime instead of my trying to convince you I'm right and you're wrong. Mere words aren't going to sway you, since you've already decided all call-in shows to psychologists are a menace to society."

"Considering them a menace would be overreacting. I simply think many such shows are exploitations."

"Mine isn't."

"Tell me why it's different while we have dinner."

"I'm not sure I'd enjoy dinner with you, since you've just insinuated to Fred Naylor and his TV audience that I might be using my radio program to hook new patients," she said flatly. "Or am I supposed to give you the benefit of the doubt and assume you weren't questioning my professional ethics?"

"Giving people the benefit of the doubt is a very healthy thing to do," was Jim's quiet answer. He looked down at her while they walked across the gold-carpeted floor. "I wasn't questioning your personal ethics and I apologize if I made it sound that way. It's just that I know that some radio psychologists are subtly encouraging some callers to make appointments with them."

"I'd never do that." Ashley observed him speculatively. "Obviously you've studied us call-in hosts pretty thoroughly. Why?"

It was almost as if a shadow passed over his face. "Long story."

"Oh."

"Have dinner with me and I might tell you about it."

She hesitated. She *was* curious, yet . . . She started to shake her head.

"You have other plans?"

"No, but—"

"That's perfect then. I don't have any, either." When she stopped in front of the bank of plate-glass doors to slip into her coat, he helped her with it, smiling. "And the food across the street is delicious. One of their specialties is sole amandine. Do you like sole?"

"Well, yes, I . . ."

Jim's smile deepened, causing shallow half-dimples to etch his lean cheeks. "Then I can highly recommend it."

He was a very persuasive man. And when Ashley's stomach rumbled, she confessed, "I am hungry."

"That settles it then," he announced, opening one of the glass doors for her, then following her out onto the sidewalk.

The mid-October air had a chill to it, but it felt crisp and smelled clean. Ashley took a deep breath and looked at Jim as they moved to the curb. Clad in black trousers and a black V-neck sweater over his shirt beneath a gray herringbone jacket, he seemed quite comfortable in the frosty night breeze that stirred strands of his sandy hair as well as tendrils of her own. He cupped her elbow in his hand when they darted across the street during a momentary lull in the busy traffic and entered the warmth of Dominique's.

After a wait at the bar, they were escorted to a cozy table for two, where they sipped their drinks and looked over the menu. Ashley chose the sole amandine and discovered Jim hadn't exaggerated. It was fantastic, and she had a healthy appetite. Lunch had been hours ago.

Talk over dinner was stimulating. Jim was an excellent conversationalist, knowledgeable about a variety of topics that Ashley was conversant in, too. One subject led to another as they exchanged opinions about politics, literature, and even next year's Super Bowl winner. Jim quoted statistics to back up his bet, but she had a favorite team and refused to be daunted by mere facts. They laughed together often. It was over coffee that Jim sat back relaxed in his chair, loosened the knot of his wine-colored tie a little and surveyed her slender hands over the rim of the cup he raised to his lips.

"No ring," he said after a moment. "You're not married, then?"

"No, never have been."

"Any special reason why not?"

"Not really. No time, I guess, to get that involved. First there was school to finish, and after that I joined Dad in his practice and found that I get very involved with my patients," Ashley said, then gave a little shrug. "Besides, I enjoy the freedom of being single. I'll probably go on unattached for a long time."

"I doubt it."

"You shouldn't. I really enjoy being on my own. But what about you? Are you married?"

"No, I never have been either."

"Any special reason why not?" she asked.

He grinned. "I guess I just haven't found the right woman yet."

"You'll have to keep looking. I'm sure she's somewhere."

"I'm sure she is."

Ashley folded her napkin neatly and placed it on the tabletop. "This has been nice, but I have some notes to go over this evening."

Without answering, Jim signaled their waiter for the check. About five minutes later they left Dominique's and Ashley wrapped her coat more snugly around herself as they went outside. The chilly breeze had picked up, and as it lifted back the arc of golden hair that grazed her right temple, she automatically smoothed it down before Jim took her arm and they hurried across the street again to the front of the building where the television studio was located. For a moment they stood in silence in the glowing circle of the streetlight.

"Dinner was wonderful," she finally said. "Thank you."

"My pleasure," he murmured, reaching out to ease one corner of her collar from inside her coat. His knuckles grazed her neck, and the touch of skin against skin was warm. "Do you need a ride home?"

"No, thank you. I have my car."

"I'll walk you to it."

After he did so, he waited until she was inside to say good night, then strode across the shadowy parking lot toward his own car. Watching him in the rearview mirror, Ashley buckled her seatbelt, inserted the key in the ignition and started the engine. As she backed out of the parking space, she realized they had scarcely discussed their professional lives during dinner. And he had never told her why he was so interested in and opposed to radio programs like hers on KTSG.

At 6:07 the following evening, right after the local news, Ashley was on the air. In the glass-enclosed cubicle from which she broadcast, she waited for the taped announcement of her program to finish before saying hello, then pushed the first flashing light at the base of her phone.

"Hello, this is Ashley. What's your name?"

There was a slight pause, fairly typical, then a faint cough over the line. "Hi . . . there, Ashley," a woman said at last. "I listen to you all the time and want you to know I wouldn't miss a minute."

"Thank you. I appreciate that," Ashley said sincerely before prompting, "What is your name? If you don't mind telling me."

"Oh no, it's Penny and I'm having a terrible time with my daughter. She's fifteen, you see, and she's impossible! She's about to make a nervous wreck out of me," the woman blurted in a rush, her voice becoming shrill. "I'm about at the end of my rope. I mean it! She acts like she can't stand me. What can I do?"

"I need to know more," Ashley told her, her tone of voice serene, calming. "What exactly do you mean when you say she's impossible?"

"She just rebels at everything, that's all! I think if I said a cow was a cow, she'd swear it was a horse. Oh, she hasn't done anything really bad . . . yet. But it seems like every little thing I say or do makes her mad."

"But you love her?"

"Of course I do! And my husband and I have done our very best for her and her two little brothers."

"She's your oldest child, then?"

"Yes."

"When did she start acting so rebellious?"

"I'm not sure. About two months ago, I guess."

"Did something happen about that time, Penny?"

There was a brief silence. "Yes, she was fifteen in August and . . ."

"And what?"

"She started pestering me to let her go out with boys."

"Hmmm, I see. And you said she couldn't?"

"I certainly did! Fifteen's too young!"

"You may think so. Obviously she doesn't. Think about that, Penny. Are you really surprised she's become rebellious in the past couple of months? When she reached fifteen, she probably thought she would be granted more privileges, but she hasn't been. She feels as if you're repressing her."

"That's not what I mean to do. I'm just trying to protect her. She's just a baby."

"A fifteen-year-old isn't a baby anymore. She's not grown up, but she's not a baby. Why are you afraid to let her be around boys, Penny? Don't you trust her?"

"Well . . . I . . ."

"Has she ever given you any reason *not* to trust her?"

"No . . . but . . ." Penny sighed heavily. "I know what it's like to be young."

"Then I'm sure you remember how it feels to start wanting to be a little more independent."

"Yes, sure, but . . ."

"Penny, I think you already know what you're going to have to do."

"Let her go?"

"Begin letting go," Ashley said. "If you don't want her to go out alone with a boy yet, maybe that should wait. But she needs some freedom. She's certainly old enough to go with a date to a party or to double-date. Be honest with yourself. Don't you think that's true?"

There was silence on the line.

"Penny?"

The woman sighed. "It's just hard for me to believe she's already fifteen."

Ashley laughed softly. "A common complaint of parents. Most of them feel time passes by too fast. But your daughter *is* fifteen. That's a fact you can't change. Understand what I'm saying?"

"Yes," Penny answered without much enthusiasm.

"Okay. Thank you for calling," Ashley said, then pressed the second light on the phone to switch to another line. "You're on the air. What's your name?"

"James. I wondered what advice you'd give me concerning my situation. I'm involved in a professional disagreement with a colleague, and it's not likely either of us is going to change our opinion."

"And this is causing friction?"

"It could."

"Before that happens, can't you reach some compromise?"

"Maybe, but in this particular situation, I doubt it."

"You're being very vague, James."

"Oh?" the male caller drawled. "Am I?"

In the glass-enclosed cubicle that was the broadcasting booth, Ashley sat back in her chair with a smile. The voice had sounded familiar from the beginning, but the inflection on that one word, *Oh?* brought instant recognition. Twirling a pencil between her fingers, she drawled back, "Since you don't seem willing to give me more details, I can't offer any concrete advice. But perhaps you should consider rethinking your position. Your colleague could be right, and it always pays to be open-minded, Jim. Thank you for calling." Without waiting for a response, she disconnected, then spoke into the microphone to her listeners. "This is Dr. Ashley Miller and we'll be back with another caller right after these messages." As a man and woman began to harmonize about the virtues of soup, especially the brand they were advertising, Ashley chuckled to herself. Jim Saxon had called, wondering what kind of advice she would give him. Now he knew.

Forty-five minutes later she left the broadcast booth while the disc jockey was reading the on-the-hour news. In the corridor she smiled at the assistant station manager, who was also her program's producer, as he hurried toward his office.

"Great show as usual," he remarked. "Good answers."

"Couldn't do it without you," she said, slipping on her jacket. "You screen the calls. See you Friday."

They exchanged good nights and Ashley walked into the lobby, humming softly. Her humming ceased abruptly when she saw Jim Saxon rising from the chair next to the unoccupied reception desk.

"This is a surprise, James," she said after a second, grinning as he approached her. "After your call, I didn't expect a visit."

He grinned back. "You didn't talk to me long enough. And your advice was too general. Since I knew you'd be here until seven, I decided to come and wait until you finished the program. I want to talk to you."

"First I have a question. How on earth did you get past Nelson, my producer—the man you talked to before you went on the air? He screens my calls, and not many people as vague as you were get past him. How did you manage it?"

"In my practice I've heard nearly every story imaginable about professional differences, so I just provided Nelson with a few convincing details. I said I suspected my colleague of trying to stab me in the back and get me fired—a very common gripe."

"You're a devious man," Ashley accused, looking at him with unveiled curiosity. "Now, tell me why you came here to talk to me. I'd hoped you would at least listen to all of my program."

"I heard the rest in the car and after I got here."

"Oh, good." Her delicately arched eyebrows lifted. "I hope that means you realize such shows aren't exploitations?"

"Yours is done in a more professional, helpful way than others I've heard," he conceded. "But I still have misgivings. That's why I'd like to talk to you. How about over dinner?"

With a comical grimace Ashley indicated with a sweeping gesture the clothes she was wearing. "I don't think jeans and a sweater are the proper attire for dining out. Thanks for asking, but I'm going to give myself a break from cooking tonight by stopping for pizza and taking it home."

"Sounds great. I like pizza. And I would like to talk to you."

The somber note in his voice made her hesitate. She tilted her head to one side inquiringly. "You make it sound very serious. Exactly what do you want to talk about?"

"Several things. Most important, the man who called you and said he was hearing voices, voices that were telling him to do things he didn't want to do. He bothered me."

The edge of Ashley's teeth sank into the full curve of her lower lip. Then she sighed. The voice-hearer bothered her, too, a great deal. And Jim had far more experience dealing with severely disturbed, perhaps psychotic people than she did. Maybe he could give her some new insights.

After a long thoughtful moment, she nodded. "All

right. Pizza at my place." She gave him her address. "See you there in half an hour. That'll give me time to pick up the pizza, then get home to make a salad."

"I have a better idea. You drive straight home and get the salad done and I'll stop for the pizza," he suggested, escorting her to the stairs that led down one flight to street level. "What kind do you like?"

"Ummm, I guess I like pepperoni best. With extra cheese."

"That's a coincidence. That's my favorite too."

As they reached the foot of the steps and started toward the street exit, Ashley glanced at him, her eyes discreetly skimming the casual navy slacks and navy crew-neck sweater he was wearing over his pale blue oxford shirt, unbuttoned at the collar. He looked attractive but quite safe; yet it wasn't like her to have dinner two nights in a row with a man she'd only just met. She was cautious, unlike her older sister, Colette, who had married twice in the past eight and a half years and was now twice divorced. Still, this situation didn't really call for caution, did it? She and Jim Saxon were only going to discuss professional matters tonight. It was like a business meeting. There was nothing whatsoever personal about it.

At least that was what she told herself as Jim walked her to her car.

CHAPTER TWO

As it turned out, Ashley and Jim didn't actually discuss professional topics during dinner. As if by mutual agreement, they talked about less serious things, which made the meal relaxing and enjoyable. Seated comfortably in the dining nook of Ashley's small house, Jim accepted another slice of pizza and refilled her glass from the bottle of red wine he had brought. His dark eyes roamed over her. She was compelling. At first glance she had seemed a totally open woman, but now he had an instinctive feeling that there were a few inhibitions hidden rather expertly in her. Maybe he was wrong. The two things he knew for certain were that she was lovely and he was attracted to her.

"Coffee?" she offered politely when the last of the pizza and salad had disappeared. "While I clear the table, you can go into the living room and I'll bring it to you. Cream? Sugar?"

"Black, please."

A few minutes later Ashley entered the living room, balancing a tray on one arm and carrying something Jim couldn't see cupped in the palm of the other. When he rose quickly from the sofa to relieve her of the burden of the tray, she smiled her thanks, then crossed the room to open the front door. A fat cat with tiger stripes and golden eyes streaked inside, looked around suspiciously, then settled a gleaming gaze on Jim.

"This is Ludlow," Ashley explained, pouring the contents of her cupped hand onto the floor before the cat. "I call him mine, but he mostly belongs to himself. I don't even see him every day, but he always seems to know to come home when I have pizza. He loves it."

"Obviously," Jim agreed, smiling as he watched Ludlow practically inhale the scraps of pepperoni and cheese Ashley had saved for him. "How old is he?"

"I don't know. I found him hanging around my back door almost two years ago. He was a stray. Looked like he hadn't had food in days. I thought he'd run away when I tried to get close to him, but he didn't. He let me pick him up and bring him inside."

"Wise cat. Judging by the weight he's gained, he knew an easy mark when he saw one," Jim said, amusement in his dark brown eyes as she wrinkled her nose at him. "You've spoiled him."

"Maybe a little, but he's a nice cat. I give him pizza once in a while, and he always comes back here. Sometimes he even gives up his wild bachelor life to spend two or three nights on the couch."

After gobbling up the last remnant of pizza, Ludlow glared at Jim once more, then stalked over to sniff his ankle. The cat's orange-toned tail flicked up twice, then he turned to go, stopping only to stretch his forepaws out, arch his back and yawn before reaching the door.

After letting him out and watching him leap across the front porch and down the steps into the darkness, Ashley closed the door behind him. Smiling, she turned back to Jim. "You see, he just drops by for pit stops."

After taking a slow sip of coffee, Jim placed the cup back on the saucer and settled himself comfortably on the sofa. She sat down at the other end, slipped her feet out of leather espadrilles and tucked them up beside her on the sofa.

"You said you still have misgivings about my radio program," she prompted after a few seconds' silence. "What exactly did you mean?"

"They're really the same misgivings I've always had. I think it might do more harm than good to allow people to believe you can solve their problems in only a few minutes. Psychological problems aren't subject to quick cures."

"And I never try to perform any. I've told you before that if I suspect the problem is a deep one, I advise professional help. Besides, as you heard tonight, most of my calls are from people with temporary troubles. Like Penny, the woman who didn't want to let her daughter start dating. I'm sure you realize she probably knew what she was going to have to do to solve that problem before she ever called me. Common sense had to tell her she needed to give the girl some freedom, but maybe she needed a little nudge from someone objective. I gave her the nudge."

"And she'll probably follow your advice. But do you think all your callers do?"

"Of course not. I hear from some very headstrong people who would rather struggle with their problems than do anything to change their attitudes or behavior. They're never wrong, and no one can convince them otherwise. They call me hoping I'll agree with them, and when I don't, they usually hang up fast. There's not much I can do for people like that except try to give them something to think about. Luckily, most of my callers are more flexible."

"Those callers aren't genuinely disturbed individuals. What about the ones who are, like the man who hears voices? That was no hoax. He sounds very close to losing all grip on reality."

"I know he does, and I've never been able to get anywhere with him," Ashley murmured, her eyes darkening with concern. "He's never even told me his name."

A pronounced frown appeared on Jim's brow. "You mean he's called you before?"

"Tonight was the fourth time. Twice I've gone off the air for a minute or so, hoping he'd talk more freely in private. All he'll say is that the voices aren't always there but when they are, they try to control him. I've begged him to go to a psychiatrist, but he says he can't."

"Maybe you're one of the reasons he feels he doesn't have to," Jim suggested, his expression hardening as he looked at her. "The fact that you're there on the radio just a phone call away may be giving him a false sense of security. By calling you, he may think he's doing something to help himself. And you're easy—he doesn't have to face you or even give you his name. For God's sake, Ashley, you shouldn't even be talking to him."

"Now hold it just a minute. That may be your professional opinion, but it isn't mine," she replied heatedly. "It could very well be I'm the only person this man can talk to. I'm sure he doesn't go telling strangers in the street he hears voices in his head. But he needs to communicate with somebody, and I can't refuse to listen to him. I have to try to persuade him to see a psychiatrist."

Jim leaned toward her, his features softening again. "Look, Ashley, I know your intentions are good," he said. "But if he believes you can solve his problem over the phone, he might not think he needs more help."

"Then, what am I supposed to do? Have Nelson tell

him to buzz off the next time he calls?" she asked calmly. "I can't risk doing that and you know it."

"Of course not. But you know how to handle people firmly yet gently. Convince him he can't use you as a crutch because that isn't going to help, at least not for long."

"If that's what he's doing," murmured Ashley, and she wasn't sure that it was. Still it had to be considered a possibility. She tapped a fingertip against her lips thoughtfully. Then her blue eyes brightened. "I have an idea. You talk to him—off the air, naturally. After all, he needs a psychiatrist instead of a psychologist anyhow. You can come to the station next Wednesday—that's the day he always calls."

"See what I'm saying? He calls on Wednesdays, like he's keeping an appointment with you. He's becoming dependent."

"Maybe you're right. He could be. But if you'd talk to him . . ."

Jim shook his head. "I can't diagnose and treat patients over the phone."

"I know you can't. I'm not asking you to do that," she persisted, a distinct note of determination in her voice. "Just talk to him. Try to get him to tell you more than he's told me. Offer to meet him somewhere. Jim, the man's crying out for help I can't give him. But maybe you can. It's worth taking the chance."

Jim didn't answer immediately. Instead he searched her face, his brown eyes intent. "You're a very persuasive woman," he said at last. "I bet you were on the college debating team."

"You're wrong. But I do have an older sister and I learned very early to think and talk fast if I wanted to win any arguments with her," Ashley told him, laughing lightly.

"And then you had all those psychology courses that taught you how to influence people with words," he teased. "That helped, too."

"You should know. You've had more of those courses than I have," she replied, laughing again. "And more experience saying just the right thing to get the results you want. But how persuasive am I? Enough to get you to come to the station Wednesday night and talk to that poor man?"

"Yes, I'll be there," he said without further hesitation. "I may not be able to help, but you're right—it's worth the chance."

She smiled warmly at him. "Thank you, Jim."

He nodded, but his gaze never left her. He was attracted to her, very strongly attracted. He liked her laugh. It was uninhibited, at variance with the professional demeanor she seemed to present to the world. And her smile was something special indeed. Not only did it curve her softly shaped lips, it also shone in the depths of her blue eyes.

Aware that he was looking at her differently, Ashley picked up her cup and took a couple of quick sips of coffee, trying to ignore the quickening beat of her heart and the warmth that stole over her body. After all, she had met many sexually appealing men; it was always an exciting but fleeting experience, a chance to indulge in a brief flirtation, and Jim was no different. He *was* sexy; she liked him, but that wasn't the point. It was time to get back to the topic at hand.

Ashley curled a strand of hair round one finger. "Last night you were going to tell me why you're so opposed to psychologist talk shows," she reminded him. "But you never did."

"As I said, it's a long story."

She spread her hands. "I've got plenty of time, and I'd like to hear it."

"I had a patient in psychoanalysis for four years. He'd suffered two severe traumas in childhood," Jim began, his eyes troubled, the set of his mouth regretful. "He was beginning to realize that those traumas were the main reason he was a disturbed adult, and we were making good progress in his therapy when his sister in California lost her husband and begged him to come live with her. It was a crucial point in his treatment, and I didn't think he should go, but he felt an obligation, which I respected. I referred him to a psychiatrist in Sacramento but found out later from his sister that he never went to the doctor there. Instead, after several weeks of listening to a radio psychologist, he decided he knew enough to cope with his illness. And a little knowledge is a dangerous thing, as the old saying goes. The last time I saw him he was in a state hospital, more disturbed than when he'd first come to me. The doctors there had written him off as hopeless, and his sister had given up on him."

Ashley sighed. She could feel Jim's pain and frustration. "I'm sorry that happened," she murmured, reaching over to touch the back of his hand and making no move to withdraw her fingers when his closed around them. "But can you really blame a radio program for everything that happened to your patient?"

"Not only to him. It's happened to others. As you said, I've made a study of this."

"Still, it must be very rare for a person to suffer a complete mental collapse because of a radio talk show."

"One's too many," Jim countered sternly. "I don't think entertaining the public is worth the productive life of even one individual. And I don't imagine you think so either."

"Put that way, you're right; I don't. But I wonder if you're being totally objective about this," she said, gently extracting her fingers from his to smooth her hair back from her face. "I'm not sure you can be that objective, since one of your patients tried to find the solution to his problem in a radio show instead of another therapist. I think you're too involved personally."

"Do you now?" Jim inquired, relaxing slightly. "Are you trying to psychoanalyze me?"

"I doubt you really need any help getting in touch with your inner feelings," she answered diplomatically. "But we all have our blind spots, don't we? We're only human."

"And you still think I'm not being objective about radio psychologists?"

"I think that's a real possibility. You might want to think it over."

"I will, but I doubt I'll change my mind."

"We'll see," Ashley said, assuming a confidence she didn't truly feel. "I think you will."

"Ah, the eternal optimist," Jim said, then pushed back the cuff of his sleeve to consult his wristwatch. He rose to his feet. "It's getting late, and we both have to get up and go to work in the morning, so I'd better be going."

Although she was disappointed that he was leaving so soon, Ashley escorted him to the door with a nonchalant smile.

Hand resting on the doorknob, he looked down at her. "Thanks for dinner."

"You brought the pizza."

"I enjoyed it."

"I did too. It was delicious."

"Good night, Ashley," he said, opening the door.

"You will be at the station Wednesday night, won't

you, Jim?" she asked as he stepped out onto the porch. "He usually calls between six-fifteen and six-twenty."

"I'll be there in plenty of time," he promised, then said good night once again.

When Ashley had closed the door behind him, then locked it, she leaned back against the solid oak and took a deep breath. She moved across the room to gather Jim's cup and saucer and her own. Before she reached the hallway leading to the kitchen, her doorbell rang, three short trills that made her hurry back across the room.

Jim stood outside her door. Cradled in his left arm was her cat. "Ludlow and I collided on the sidewalk," he explained. "He was obviously on his way back here but I didn't see him in the shadows. I stepped on one of his paws and he let out a yowl. Thought you'd better take a look at him to be sure he's okay."

Ludlow seemed just fine, judging by the way he was twisting and squirming and trying to snake out of Jim's hands while Ashley checked his paws. "He's all right. You can put him down," she said, smiling indulgently as the cat zipped across the living room heading toward the kitchen. "The only thing bothering him is the nip in the air. He does stay home a lot more when the weather gets cold."

"It is chilly tonight. You'd better go back in," said Jim. He started to turn away, then paused and looked back at her. "Have dinner with me Friday evening at my house."

"I can't," she told him honestly. "I already have plans."

"Busy Saturday night, too?"

"As a matter of fact, I'm not."

"Good. I'll pick you up at seven. And I'm not going to take no for an answer."

Before she could respond, he was leaving, striding across the lawn toward his car. Slowly she shut the door and smiled. She hadn't intended to say no anyway.

On Saturday morning Ashley liked to sleep late, usually until nine-thirty or ten. The shrill ringing of her phone interrupted a pleasant dream, and she forced her eyes open. When she saw it was barely eight o'clock, she was tempted to stick her head under the pillow, but she didn't. All her patients had her home phone number. She knew it could be one of them but hoped it wasn't. She needed a break. Last night's session with the Monroe family had been long and tension-filled. It had been a hectic week, and she wanted some time to herself. But the phone just kept ringing. Yawning, she picked up the receiver and mumbled a hello.

"Are you still in bed?" her father's teasing voice came back. "Don't you know it's time to be up and about?"

"No and I don't want to know it," she retorted sleepily. "You know I sleep late on Saturdays so this better be good, Dad."

"Well, I thought you might like to know your name's in this morning's paper."

"Oh, drat. The police promised me they'd keep the story quiet."

"I'm not kidding," Tom Miller replied. "Your name is in the paper."

"I can't imagine why. What's it all about?"

"Jim Saxon mentions you in an article they did about him."

"Oh, he did?" Ashley murmured, her tone guarded. Running her fingers through her tousled hair, she sat up in bed. "What did he say about my program?"

"Well, if it's a compliment, I think it's a back-handed

one. But your mother says I'm just being overly sensitive. Want me to read you the quote?"

"I don't think I'm ready to hear it right at the moment. I'll just get up, bring in the paper, and read the whole article. And I might as well do it now, since I'm wide awake," she complained halfheartedly. "I could have slept a couple of hours longer."

"You'll never miss two hours. What you should do is jog around the block. Get your blood circulating."

"It's circulating just fine, thank you, and the last thing in the world I want to do is go jogging. What I need is a cup of coffee, so I'll talk to you later, Dad, okay? Hello to Mom. Does she still want me for lunch tomorrow?"

"Yes, and Colette's coming too. Maybe you can cheer her up a little. This postdivorce depression of hers doesn't seem to be getting much better."

"Umm, I know. I talked to her yesterday. But try not to worry. Remember what you'd tell any of your patients: these things take time."

"You're right."

"As always," she said teasingly, then said good-bye. Reluctantly she pushed back the warm covers, slipped out of bed and quickly donned her velour robe. She stepped into fuzzy slippers before venturing out the front door and across the porch to the top step, where the newspaper had mercifully landed. Shivering in the nearly freezing morning air, she rushed back inside, went into the kitchen to plug in the percolator, then began to scan the newspaper for the article about Jim. She found it in the first section, and her eyes were immediately drawn to the photo of him. It was a good one. Sitting back in his chair behind his desk, he looked approachable yet serious, warm yet professional. Then the headline claimed her attention: LOCAL PSYCHIATRIST

SEES DANGERS IN POP PSYCHOLOGY. Groaning softly, she began to read. His opinion of radio psychologists was made quite clear. She came to his reference to her: "Even programs like the one here in Boulder, 'Let's Talk,' hosted very professionally and without a titillating emphasis on sex by Dr. Ashley Miller, worry me. I'm afraid all shows like this give the public the impression that there's an easy solution to every problem, which isn't true."

After folding the paper, Ashley laid it on the countertop. "You're right, Dad," she said aloud. "That's a very back-handed compliment." *If it could be considered a compliment at all.* She was sure it couldn't. Jim was focusing only on the negative possibilities involved in call-in programs to psychologists. He wasn't considering the possible benefits. Pouring a cup of steaming coffee, she decided she was just going to have to try to change his mind. But how?

At almost seven o'clock on the dot that evening, Jim arrived at Ashley's house. When she answered his knock and opened the door, his gaze swept discreetly over her, taking in every curving contour covered but not concealed by the simply designed forest-green jersey dress she wore. Its loosely gathered skirt and obi sash tied around her narrow waist were both demure and sensuous at the same time.

"I just have to get my coat," she told him after he stepped in to the house and closed the door behind him.

He watched her walk over to the sofa, where she'd left her coat. "Where's old Ludlow?" he asked conversationally. "Chilly as it is tonight, I expected to find him curled up on a chair."

"He's still out prowling around." Ashley smiled her thanks when Jim came over to hold her coat as she slipped her arms into the sleeves. "But he'll probably be waiting on the doorstep when I get back. He doesn't care much for winter. He's more a summer cat."

"How about you?" Jim asked, straightening her collar, allowing his knuckles to graze her neck. "Are you a summer or a winter person?"

Feeling far too aware of his touch, she took a small step back, putting more distance between them. "I like summer and winter both."

"Then you probably ski?"

"Whenever I get a chance. I only got to go once last winter, but I'm planning to hit the slopes more often this year. I need the exercise."

"I can't tell," he said, a warm glow of amusement lighting his brown eyes as he looked her over with deliberate slowness. "You look in very good shape to me."

"Thanks for saying so, but I'm not sure I should take you seriously. After all, this morning my very own father advised me to start jogging," she said, then swiftly switched the subject. "And by the way, Dad thought your comment about me in this morning's paper was a back-handed compliment."

"Ah, you did see that. I thought you would."

"I did, and—"

"No shop talk tonight," he interrupted gently, placing one long, lean finger against her lips to silence her words. "This is going to be strictly a social evening. I think it's time we got to know each other better . . . personally."

His slight emphasis on that last word made Ashley's heart skip a beat, but she went willingly with him as he escorted her out of the house to the ivory Volvo parked in the driveway.

Jim drove southwest out of Boulder, and as mile after mile passed, Ashley turned in her seat to rest her arm over the back and smile at him. "And I thought I lived far from the city. Where exactly *do* you live? Somewhere in the state of Colorado, I presume?"

Jim laughed. "It's not much farther. I live just this side of Nederland."

"Oh, that's a lovely place. I've always liked to drive through that area. It's like a different world compared to town."

"It's my hideaway," he murmured, glancing over at her for a long moment before concentrating exclusively on the winding road.

About ten minutes later Jim turned off the highway onto a narrower road that climbed the hills in serpentine curves. Bare rock faces interspersed with thickets of trees mirrored the reflection of the Volvo's headlights, and Ashley gazed out her window, awed as usual by the sheer majesty of nature's undisturbed wonder. Stately evergreens towered above, etched in silhouette against the moonlit sky. When Jim turned again, onto a sinuously curving drive that led through a copse of aspen trees nearly stripped of their leaves and surrounded by a band of ponderosa pines, Ashley sat straighter in her seat, waiting expectantly. In a clearing, Jim's house stood, a long cedar and hewn rock structure with a stone chimney that rose two stories high, obviously providing a fireplace for the upstairs room as well as the one below it. Ashley immediately fell in love with the place.

"Jim, it's beautiful," she whispered as he stopped the car and shut off the engine. Silence enveloped them, the silence of unfettered nature and peaceful seclusion. Dragging her eyes from the picturesque scene, she looked at him. "Oh, I can see why it's your hideaway. I love it."

They got out of the car. Cupping her elbow in one hand, he directed her along the flagstone walk and up a step to the wooden deck of the house. They went in and he switched on the foyer light, watching Ashley as she looked all around, observing the walnut deacon's bench to her left, the oval mirror above it, and the brightly colored primitive paintings on the opposite wall.

"I'll take your coat," Jim said, and as he was hanging it up, she stepped down into the great room. A royal blue oval area rug warmed the polished hardwood floor, and the comfortable-looking rust-and-blue tattersall plaid sofa and chairs facing the stone fireplace were simply designed. One wall was lined with books from floor to ceiling.

"I like this," Ashley told Jim when he joined her. "It's so spacious but cozy."

Looking down at her, he grinned. "Is that a nice way of saying it looks lived-in?"

"In a way. That's why I like it. I think homes should look lived-in." She sniffed appreciatively. "Something smells delicious. What are you making?"

"Saxon's famous roast chicken supreme. The recipe's a secret," he said, motioning her toward a chair. "Have a seat. Dinner'll be ready in a few minutes. Would you like a drink while you're waiting?"

"No thanks. I'd be happy to help you in the kitchen."

"There's nothing much left to do, but you could get a fire going in here while I take the chicken out. The matches are on the mantel."

After he left the room, she kneeled on the raised hearth. Several good-size logs were already arranged in the fireplace with enough kindling beneath to make starting a fire as easy as striking the match. Soon flames were licking upward, crackling as the bark on the logs began to burn away, and she remained there watching their swaying dance and basking in the warmth.

"I've always loved sitting in front of a fireplace," she

murmured a few minutes later when Jim touched her shoulder. Looking up at him, she began to stand.

"No, don't get up," he softly commanded. "We'll eat here by the fire, use the hearth as a table." Stepping away from her, he took some throw pillows from the sofa and chairs and tossed them on the floor. "But I think we'll be much more comfortable sitting on these."

Dinner was delicious. There was indeed something special about the chicken and the stuffing he had made to go with it, a subtle, tantalizing taste she couldn't identify.

"I'd love to know what you did to this chicken," she said after finishing everything on her plate. She took a sip of chilled white wine. "I think you added some rare herb or spice. What was it?"

Jim shook his head. "That's the secret. My grandmother practically made me swear I wouldn't give anyone the recipe. I guess she was afraid it might get back to one of her women friends. It's her one secret recipe, and she plans to keep it that way. Grandpa says she'd probably divorce him if he ever let the secret ingredients slip. He loves to tease her."

Jim's fond tone made Ashley smile. "You sound like you're very close to your grandparents."

"I am. They were always close by when I was a kid. My parents' house is only a couple of hundred yards from theirs. They run a cattle ranch just south of Colorado Springs."

Ashley's eyes widened. "You were raised on a cattle ranch?"

"That always seems to surprise people," he said wryly, propping his elbow on one of the throw cushions and stretching out his long legs. "But even psychiatrists have to come from somewhere. I came from a ranch."

"What made you decide to go into psychiatry?"

"I was always more interested in medicine than ranching. I didn't decide to specialize in psychiatry until I was an intern."

"Where'd you go to medical school?"

"Harvard."

"Hmmm, such a long way from home."

"You can say that again." Jim laughed. "The school of medicine is in Boston, and I felt like a country bumpkin there until I got used to it."

"I can't imagine you ever being a country bumpkin."

"Oh, I can assure you I wasn't always the debonair man about town I am now," he joked, shaking his head. "And I was homesick. I missed my family and the ranch and peace and quiet. That's why I built this place way out here in the woods. I needed some space to myself. I'm still a country boy at heart, I guess."

"Do you have brothers and sisters?" Ashley asked, curious about him, wanting to know more about his background.

"One sister, one brother. Evelyn's married and lives in Oregon. Mark is single and still lives on the ranch."

"Are they younger or older?"

"I'm the oldest," he told her, his deep brown eyes capturing and holding hers. "And what about you? I know your father's a psychologist and you're in practice with him. Any siblings?"

Ashley wrinkled her nose at him, then had to laugh. "Your profession's showing, Dr. Saxon. Only a psychiatrist would use the word *sibling.*"

He chuckled, easily able to laugh at himself. "You're right, so I'll rephrase the question. Do you have brothers and sisters?"

"One sister—Colette. She's three years older than me."

"Aha, vell then, perhaps *sibling* was ze appropriate

word after all," he suggested, pretending to stroke an imaginary beard while affecting a German accent. "Two daughters only three years apart must have experienced some of ze most intense sibling rivalries."

"Mom says we fought like cats and she was tempted more than once to throw us both out of the house," Ashley admitted, a reminiscent smile curving her lips. "She tried to boss me around, and I resented it. I didn't have to do as much around the house because I was the baby, and she resented that. We had some rip-roaring squabbles and hurled insults at each other you wouldn't believe. Fortunately, we both grew up and now we act much more civilized."

"You're friends?"

"Yes. We talk on the phone three or four times a week and see each other at least once. Lately it's been more often. She's going through her second divorce and naturally that's rough, so she needs all the support Mom and Dad and I can give her."

Jim's gaze narrowed as he continued to hold hers. "And you're a very supportive person."

"I'm supposed to be, in my profession."

"Which you're very good at, I'm sure."

She tilted her head to one side inquiringly. "Except, you mean, when it comes to my call-in program?"

"I think that is a waste of your talent and training. But we aren't going to get into a discussion about that tonight. Remember? This is our time to get better acquainted," he murmured. "So where did you go to school?"

Ashley told him, and as they shared memories of their pasts, time slipped away with incredible speed. The flames in the fireplace died; the logs were becoming smoldering embers, and when the top one collapsed on the others with a thud and a shower of sparks, Ashley's gaze moved from Jim to the dying fire, then back to him again. When he slowly reached over and drew his fingertips over the back of her hand, pleasurable sensations rushed over her. Too pleasurable. At that moment he seemed a very dangerous man, and she pulled her hand away as discreetly as possible to start gathering their plates and emptied wineglasses. "I'll help you tidy up before you take me home," she announced, rising gracefully to her feet. "I even volunteer to wash dishes in return for a delicious dinner."

A faint knowing smile moved Jim's mouth as he too stood to look down at her. "You don't have to do that. I'll just put them into the dishwasher when I get back."

"All right. But at least let me take these into the kitchen," she insisted, then turned and walked slowly away from him.

Nearly thirty minutes later they arrived at her house. As she had predicted, they found Ludlow huddled on the front porch, and he meowed plaintively at them as if to say, "What were you doing in front of a warm fire when you knew I was here, freezing to death?"

Ashley forced herself to ignore his whining protest. After finding her key in the bottom of her purse, where it always managed to burrow, she unlocked her front door, opened it and stepped inside. She turned to Jim. "Would you like some coffee?"

He shook his head. "No, thanks."

"I enjoyed dinner. I just wish you could give me the recipe for that chicken."

"I'll have to get permission from Grandma."

"Tell her I'll never tell a soul," Ashley said, smiling. "Well . . . good night, Jim."

"Good night," he responded, then leaned down to lightly kiss her, but as her softly shaped lips yielded to the slight pressure of his, all his inner resolve flew right out the window.

Ashley's breath caught as he stepped close, one muscular arm slipping around her waist as he kissed her again. This time it was much more than a chaste peck. His warm mouth, descending swiftly on hers, gently parted her lips, and as a hot thrill rushed through her, she kissed him back for several exhilarating seconds before coming to her senses. Much as she liked and admired Jim, she didn't really know him very well, and it simply wasn't like her to allow herself to be swept off her feet. She tensed in his embrace, turned her face aside and stepped back, away from him, trying to ignore the shiver that feathered up and down her spine as her eyes met his.

"Ashley," he whispered, brushing the edge of one thumb along her jawline. "It's a long, cold drive back to my house."

"But you'll make it without any trouble," she whispered back. "All you have to do is turn the heater on full blast. That should keep you warm enough."

He had to laugh, then tap the end of her nose with one fingertip as he asked, "How did I know you were going to say something like that?"

"Because you're a very perceptive person, as a psychiatrist should be," she flatly replied despite the smile that was twitching at the corners of her mouth. "Good night, Jim. See you Wednesday night at the radio station."

After Ludlow careened around his feet to get into the house, Jim stepped back. "Wednesday night," he agreed, and after she closed the door gently, he walked back to his car. He started the engine, then watched as Ashley pulled down the shades of her two front windows. Shifting into reverse, he backed out of her driveway, but his thoughts were still of her when he braked at a stop sign a few minutes later. Outwardly she was cool and all professional, but her fleetingly ardent response to his kiss indicated to him that fires of passion smoldered beneath that deceptive exterior. And attracted to her as he was, he wanted to ignite those fires. He wanted to see desire for him illuminating her lovely blue eyes.

CHAPTER THREE

Ashley's program was nearly over Wednesday evening, and the man who said he heard voices still hadn't called. He was later than usual, and that concerned her. Inside the broadcast booth, she stared out the glass partition at Nelson, who was manning the outside line. Jim sat patiently beside him, ready to try to talk to the man if he finally did phone. Nibbling a fingernail, she only half heard the string of commercials as she watched Nelson answer the phone again. But this time was different. He gave a nod, and as Jim took the call on another extension, she breathed a sigh of relief. Then the last commercial jangled to a finish and she had to go on the air again to concentrate on the particular problem of the evening's last caller.

A few minutes later, when she left the booth, she found Jim standing outside the door waiting. Her eyes darted up to his face but his expression was unreadable, giving her no indication of how the phone call had gone.

"Any luck?" she asked, hope lighting her features. "Would he talk to you at all?"

"He didn't talk long but he said enough," was Jim's cryptic answer. "You won't be hearing from your voice-hearer again."

"But—how can you be sure of that? Did he agree to see you for treatment?"

"No. When I told him who I was and that you'd asked me to talk to him, he laughed. For quite a long time, as a matter of fact," Jim told her dryly. "Then he said and I quote, 'I really had her going, didn't I? I knew I could convince her I was freaking out. The guys in my frat bet me I couldn't.' "

"It was just a hoax, then," she murmured, shaking her head and giving in to a wry smile. "Well, thank heavens. I was afraid some poor soul was being tortured by mental voices and wasn't able to reach out for help. I'm so glad this man was just putting me on. And he's right—he certainly did have me going."

"I'm surprised you're not a little upset," Nelson said, joining in the conversation. "Don't you resent being tricked?"

Ashley shrugged. "When your job is listening to people, you take the chance of having some of them lie to you."

"Well, this guy certainly pulled the wool over everybody's eyes. Since the first time he called you, we've been hearing from listeners who've been very worried about him."

"Now we'll be able to ease their minds. At the beginning of Friday night's program, I'll tell our listeners that we've all been conned, that our voice-hearer was just a college boy pulling a prank."

Frowning, Nelson began working his mouth from side to side, a habit of his whenever he was thinking hard. He shook his head. "I don't know if you want to tell our audience that or not, Ashley," he said. "In fact, I'm pretty sure we shouldn't. If you admit one of your callers fooled you into believing he was practically psychotic, we'll probably start hearing from copycats all over town who want to see if they can fool you too."

"That's another chance we'll have to take," Ashley

stated flatly. "Because I'm going to tell my listeners the truth about what happened. I'm not about to let any of them going on worrying about a terribly disturbed person who never existed."

"But if you tell the truth, you might be risking your own credibility," Nelson argued, shaking his head even more vehemently. "Our listeners want you to be all-knowing."

"Which I'm not. And I want them to know that. I never claimed to be a miracle worker or a prophet. I'm just a trained psychologist. I've studied human behavior, and if the people who call are honest with me, I give them advice to help them solve their problems. But if I expect them to be honest with me, I have to be honest with them, too, so I'm going to tell them the truth."

"I don't think you should."

"I realize that, but I'm still going to."

"But—"

"Nelson, either I tell them I was hoodwinked by a mischievous college kid or you're going to have to find another psychologist to do this program," she declared firmly. "That's just the way it is."

"All right, all right, you win." Nelson heaved a sigh, put his hands up, then gave her a quick peck on the cheek. "You know I don't want to find another psychologist. Our audience loves you, and if we're lucky, we won't get too many crank calls after you make your on-the-air confession." He turned to Jim and extended a hand. "Nice to meet you, Doc. Gotta run now—piles of paperwork on my desk."

After Nelson said good night and scurried away, Ashley looked over at Jim again. His expression was still inscrutable, and she wondered what he was thinking as they walked across the station lobby together.

"Well, what else did our campus comedy king tell

you?" she asked, amusement accentuating the lilt in her voice. "Is he a drama major? If he isn't, he should be. The way he breathed, 'I hear these voices, whispery voices that are telling me to do—*things,*' over and over certainly sent a chill through me. And after you heard him last week, you thought he was genuinely ill too."

"Yes, I did." In the hall that led to the stairs, Jim stopped abruptly to lightly grasp her upper arms and turn her toward him. "Which simply proves my point, Ashley: during a radio program that's little more than another form of entertainment, you can't get close to the people you talk to. Over the phone they can hide too much. And they can lie, like this kid did. Over the phone you weren't able to see his face, to look for the signals that might have told you he wasn't telling the truth. Do you see what I mean?"

"I see," she muttered, tensing, her eyes going a glacier blue. "This is your way of saying I told you so, isn't it?"

"If you want to put it that way," he replied, dropping his hands, his own gaze cooling. "I do think what happened tonight proves my point: you can't do much to help people with their problems when the only contact you have with them is a few minutes on the phone."

"I don't agree. Almost everybody who calls me has a minor problem that I can help with. Oh, sure, I'm going to get crank calls once in a while, but even if I do, that doesn't mean my whole program's worthless. And I'm not going to quit just because I might have to put up with a few comedians."

"What about the other side of the coin?" Jim asked. "I wonder how often you talk to callers who make their situations sound far less serious than they are. You know as well as I do that many people try to conceal a great deal. And if they aren't giving you adequate information, your pat answers can't help them," he said angrily.

"I don't give pat answers. I listen and I try to steer my callers in the right direction," Ashley tersely replied, starting down the steps at the end of the hall. "If we're going to argue about this again, let's do it over coffee. There's a café down the street about half a block."

"Not tonight. My first patient tomorrow is in early analysis and she's very hostile," Jim said, stopping beside her at the foot of the stairs. "I'm meeting her husband in half an hour. Hopefully he can give me a little insight."

"You'd better get going, then," Ashley murmured, trying to ignore the twinge of disappointment she felt because he had to leave. She pushed open the outside door and stepped onto the sidewalk. An icy gust of wind blew her hair across her face, and she had to fight it back to add, "Good night, Jim."

"I'll walk you to your car."

"No. I—have to run across the street to the drugstore first," she said, moving toward the curb. "You go on. We can talk about this later."

"Yes," was all he said, lifting the collar of his jacket up around his neck as he strode away.

"Sorry tonight was a waste of your time," she called after him.

"No problem," he called back, then disappeared around the corner of the building.

Ashley took a deep breath and shivered as frigid air filled her lungs. Wrapping her coat more snugly around her, she walked across the street to the drugstore, where she purchased a bottle of shampoo she needed and a chocolate bar she didn't need but wanted anyhow. Driving home, she munched on it and tried to dismiss the vague sense of disappointment that still lingered.

After dinner out with Colette Friday evening, Ashley went home alone. Ludlow was waiting for her on the front step. She let him into the house, and he made a beeline for his bowl, refueled, then took off into the night again. Ashley went to her room, where she gladly got out of her suit and slipped into her most comfortable jeans and a sweater. Padding barefoot into the living room, she switched on the television, finding a comedy show that she usually liked. Just as she curled up comfortably in a chair and started to pick up her embroidery, there was a knock on the door. Drawing a deep breath, she got up, hoping the unexpected visitor wouldn't be Norman from down the street. Barely sixteen, he was suffering through a rough adolescence complicated by a spotty complexion and he seemed to believe her main purpose in life was to be his always-available counselor. She liked Norman; he was a nice kid, but toward the end of the week, he could be a bit trying.

Before turning the key in the lock, she called out, "That you, Norman?"

"No," a deep voice called back. "Sorry to disappoint you but it's just me, Jim."

Just Jim. She would never have described him like that. With a little rush of excitement she unlocked the door and opened it, smiling softly.

"Maybe I shouldn't have come without calling first but I was on my way home and decided to take a little detour and come see you," he explained, leaning on one hand against the doorjamb. "I hope you don't mind me just dropping by?"

"No, of course not. Please come in," she said, stepping aside. She didn't mind his dropping by, but she was surprised. When they'd parted Wednesday night at the radio station, she had gotten the impression he was bored not only with her call-in program but with her personally. She really hadn't expected to see him again. When he moved past her, she detected the clean, faint fragrance of his woodsy after-shave. She motioned him toward the sofa.

"Who's Norman?" he asked, unbuttoning his gray pinstripe jacket as he sat down. "Are you sure I'm not disturbing you? If you're expecting somebody . . ."

"I don't have to expect Norman; he just comes. He's a teenager who lives three houses down, and whenever his parents or his little sister get on his nerves, which is often, he heads here, since I'm the only psychologist in the neighborhood."

"And maybe there's another reason he likes to come," Jim suggested matter-of-factly. "Could be he's a little infatuated with you."

"Oh, I thought about that, then ruled it out." Ashley laughed softly. "Norman thinks of me as old; after all, I'm ten years older than he is. I'm a member of his parents' generation but a better listener, according to him."

"You may be twenty-six but you're not exactly doddering yet, and sixteen-year-old males are very susceptible."

Ashley's spine stiffened. "You have a habit of questioning my judgment, don't you?"

"Bad day?" he inquired, reaching out to take her hand and draw her down beside him before releasing her fingers. "If it was, I can certainly sympathize. I've had better myself. The patient I told you about—the extremely hostile one—is fighting analysis like hell. Daily sessions aren't helping; she won't allow herself to trust me yet. If your day was anything like mine, I can understand why you took what I said the wrong way. I wasn't being judgmental, just objective, Ashley."

She relaxed and heaved a sigh. "It hasn't been a red-letter day exactly. I have a patient who's a genius at refusing to admit he deliberately sabotages every close relationship he has with women. And at dinner . . ." she began, then shook her head. "Let's just say I've had many much better days. And since yours wasn't such a hot one either, why don't I get you a drink? I have some very good brandy."

"No thanks. I still have the long drive home."

"Coffee, then?"

"I'm fine. Except . . ." He began loosening his tie. "I'll be much more comfortable when I get this off. You don't mind?"

"Heavens no, be my guest," she said, watching as he removed the tie completely, then unfastened his collar button. He took off his coat and rolled up the sleeves of his white shirt, exposing strong, broad wrists and subtly muscled forearms.

"Ah, that's better," he declared, a smile playing over his lips. "The civilized world certainly has many advantages, but I've decided having to wear business suits isn't one of them."

"I know a few women who feel the same way about high-heeled shoes."

"I can see why. Those things look like torture devices. Don't they kill your feet?"

"You get used to them. I guess it's a matter of conditioning. I love shoes," Ashley confessed, turning to sit sideways on the sofa, her legs tucked up beside her. "I can resist almost anything more than a pair of shoes that catches my fancy. That's my one real weakness."

Jim's dark brown eyebrows lifted. "You only have one?"

"Where money's concerned, one's about all I can afford, since really nice shoes cost so much these days."

"What about the weaknesses that have nothing to do with money? You must have some of those. We all do."

"Oh, I do have my share," she agreed, smiling. "For one, I have a hard time resisting chocolate bars. And I have a weakness for stray dogs and cats; I feed every one that comes around. Ludlow proves that."

Silently Jim looked at her, trying to search the depths of her lovely blue eyes. In many ways she was a very open person, yet there was still much about her he didn't know, her inner feelings and most secret thoughts. He wanted her to share those with him, not because he was a psychiatrist and seeking insight into personalities was his profession. He needed to know all about her for strictly personal reasons.

Ashley's breathing quickened slightly as he continued to look at her without saying a word. At last she had to break the silence. "What about you? I've told you some of my weaknesses. It's only fair for you to tell me some of yours."

A slow smile moved his mouth, carving those attractive half-dimples in his cheeks. "All right, if you must know, I'm a roasted-peanut addict. And I can't eat just a few at a time. Once I start, I can't stop until they're all gone."

"I thought it was potato chips that affected people like that."

He spread his hands in a resigned gesture. "Well, I have a minor problem with them, too."

She had to laugh. "Any other shocking weaknesses?"

"A few. Mysteries, for instance. I always have to try to solve them," he said, his tone lowering as he observed her closely. "And you sounded very mysterious a while ago when you were telling me about your day. You started to tell me something that happened at dinner, then you stopped, and I can't help wondering what you were going to say. Care to solve this mystery for me?"

Ashley's smile faded and she sighed softly while sweeping her fingers through her hair. "It's really not a mystery. I had dinner with Colette—she's my sister," she explained. "I told you, didn't I, that she's going through her second divorce?"

"Yes."

"Some days are better for her than others," Ashley continued. "Today happened to be one of her worst. She was on the verge of tears all during dinner and hardly ate anything. I wanted to go home with her just to keep her company, but she said she needed to be alone. I understand that feeling, but understanding doesn't stop me from worrying about her. She's much more upset this time than she was when her first marriage failed."

"A natural reaction. Two tries—no successes. That has to be discouraging."

"Of course. But she says she feels like a total failure. Her self-esteem is so low, almost nonexistent. She blames herself for the breakup of both marriages although she shouldn't. It wasn't all her fault that it didn't work out either time. Her first husband was selfish and immature, and the second, Eric, was so rigid and opinionated that it was impossible to have a reasonable discussion with him unless you agreed with his every word. Colette made her big mistake when she got involved too quickly with both men and made a commitment before she really knew either one of them. But she doesn't see it that way. She believes some lack in her caused her marriages to fail. And she seems to be drifting into a deepening depression. That really concerns me."

"Is she seeing a counselor?" Jim inquired. "Someone other than you or your father, I mean."

"I've tried to convince her to go to somebody, but she always laughs that suggestion off. She says that with two psychologists in the family, she doesn't need to talk to a stranger."

"So she talks to you and your father instead?"

"To me. But not to Dad. She thinks he's terribly disappointed in her for being such a poor judge of character, *twice.*"

"Is he disappointed?"

"Maybe a little," Ashley conceded, her shoulders rising and falling in a slight shrug. "But he's personally involved in this situation; she's his daughter, and he's only human."

"And you're only human too, Ashley," Jim quietly reminded her, slipping across the sofa to take both her hands in his. "You're personally involved. You can't give Colette objective advice . . . even though she might be hoping you can help her find answers to her problems, the way you do your patients."

Sighing once more, Ashley nodded. "You're very perceptive. Colette does seem to want to believe I'll come up with some magic solution for her."

"Which makes you feel guilty because you can't?"

"Not guilty, really. Just frustrated. Intellectually I know she has to be counseled by someone totally objective. But emotionally I wish so much that I could come up with the solution she needs," Ashley said, tears that had been threatening all evening suddenly glimmering in her eyes. "Oh, damn, it hurts to see someone you love in pain."

"Yes, it does, but we both know that when it comes to

members of the family, about all we can do is give love and support," Jim murmured back, his right hand coming up to cup her jaw. With his thumb he brushed away the teardrop that had caught in the thick fringe of her lower lashes before it could spill onto the faint violet crescent of skin beneath her eye. His fingertips moved soothingly over the side of her neck. "As you said, we can't be objective when dealing with those closest to us. So you're going to have to persuade Colette to talk to someone who isn't personally involved. Tell her the truth, Ashley. Convince her you're too close to her to fairly explore what went wrong with her marriages."

Imprisoned by his dark gaze, Ashley nodded. "I am going to have to insist, and I can, because we always try to be candid with each other. Even though she's feeling vulnerable and unsure of herself right now, she's really strong. With a little help, she's going to be all right."

"If she's anything like you, I'm sure she will be," said Jim softly, grazing his fingertips over the nape of her neck. "Although you're something of a puzzle yourself. Sometimes you're so cool and professional, and then at other times you show how tenderhearted you are, an adopter of scruffy stray cats other people would probably chase out of their yards. You're a fascinating woman, Ashley. Did you know that?"

She couldn't answer because as his free hand slowly glided around her waist to rest at the small of her back and he drew her slowly toward him, everything changed. Her heart seemed to take a crazy little downward dip when she recognized the glow of light in his brown eyes. Suddenly the lamp seemed softer and the wind that rustled the last of the autumn leaves seemed a gentle whisper. Jim lowered his head and his lean face filled her vision. Her breath caught sharply in her throat when his firm, warm lips touched hers, then the corners of her mouth, again and again. She trembled.

"Jim, don't. I . . ."

"Hush," he softly beseeched, taking her in his arms, holding her closer. "Ashley, let me really kiss you. Open your mouth a little."

"Jim, I . . ." she began, then obeyed, her soft lips parting beneath the swiftly graduating pressure exerted by his. A pulsating quiver of sensual delight ran through her as his warm mouth sought to take total possession of her own and his muscular arms bound her nearer. Unable to think rationally, she slipped her own arms around him. When he pulled her onto his lap, she was powerless to resist; being close to him felt too good, and the caressing movement of his hands over her back was too exciting. Then the tip of his tongue pushed gently between her lips into her mouth, finding hers, feathering over it, sending wild tremors over every inch of her skin. Pressing against him, she stroked the strong, tanned column of his neck with fluttering fingertips as his kisses lengthened and deepened and she kissed him back. Her heart thundered against her breasts. Waves of heat suffused her body, and her tongue tangled in an erotic dance with his.

She tasted like honey. Aroused by her sweetness, by the ample curves of her slender body, and by her ardent response, Jim tightened his arms with gentle fierceness around her, the beat of his heart accelerating rapidly as her breasts yielded to his chest. He ran his fingers through her silky hair, and his lips left hers only to scatter kisses over her cheeks, the delicate line of her jaw and the length of her neck. "Ashley," he murmured huskily.

Tangling her fingers in his thick hair, she urged his mouth back up to her own, the soft rush of her breath mingling with his. Their lips touched and parted again and again, nuzzling, caressing. Touching him was such pleasure. She grazed the tips of her thumbs along the rims of his ears before exploring the inner contours and, as one large firm hand followed the line of her hip upward to her insweeping waist, then upward still more, her arms wound around his neck. His palm cupped the side of one breast, moving in slow, evocative circles against taut, uprising flesh, long fingers curving around her back to hold her while he nibbled tenderly at one earlobe.

Succumbing to growing delight, she parted her lips wider to the impassioned pressure of his. Her swiftly indrawn breath was audible when he slid his hand beneath her sweater, his fingertips gliding purposely up across her bare midriff. Upon her breasts, his touch was fiery, seeming to sear her skin through the sheer, lacy fabric of her bra, and she pressed her nails down against the corded muscle of his shoulders as he probed her firm, rounded flesh inch by inch, then played his thumbs over and around the summits, arousing them to hard tips that strained against fabric.

"You feel so good," he groaned, cupping one breast in his palm. "I want you."

His intentions were clear, but her feelings were suddenly mixed. Physically she wanted him, too, but emotionally . . . With reluctance she made herself cover his hand with hers and still his fingers when he started to unfasten the closure of her bra. "No, Jim."

"No?"

"No," she quietly repeated, looking into his eyes when he held her slightly away from him. She shook her head. "Things just happened too fast, got a little bit out of control. But I really don't want to get involved this way."

"With me, you mean?"

"With anybody."

"Why, Ashley?" he asked solemnly, brushing his knuckles with feather lightness over her cheek. "You don't want to get involved because Colette's had bad luck with men?"

"That isn't the reason," she answered. She paused a second to reconsider, then qualified that statement. "Well, maybe her bad experiences have had something to do with the way I feel, but mainly I'm very happy with my life the way it is and I don't want to change it. Besides, I'm so busy with the radio program and patients and family that I hardly have any time to myself as it is. And I'm a person who needs time alone."

"But you're not a loner," Jim murmured, drawing a fingertip along her face.

Still far too disturbed by his touch, she slipped from his embrace to move a few inches away from him on the sofa, tugged the hem of her sweater more snugly over her hips, then smoothed back her hair. "Of course I'm not a loner. Far from it. I like being with other people and I almost always am with someone."

"In your profession you have to be. But what about your personal life? Maybe you're making the same mistake so many therapists make when they first start out; maybe you're letting your patients and their problems become your whole existence," Jim said. "Be careful, Ashley. You can't go on that way very long without beginning to lose your own identity."

"I know all about that pitfall, but it's not my problem, really. My patients aren't my entire life. I have close friends, my family."

"And you're also a healthy young woman, so is that enough?"

Ashley stared at him. "Are *you* trying to psychoanalyze *me* this time?"

"No. This is personal, and I'm just trying to understand why you're afraid to get involved with a man—with me."

"I'm not afraid. I want to get involved . . . someday. Right now I'm just too busy for a romantic entanglement."

"Did I suggest a romantic entanglement?" he inquired flatly. "Maybe all I wanted was a one-night stand."

Her gaze narrowed as she stared at him. "Is that all you wanted?"

"What do you think?"

She didn't know. He was such an enigma. He didn't seem to be a superficial man, one who could find much real gratification in mere casual sex. Yet she didn't really know him all that well. Maybe he wasn't as sensitive as he appeared. And if all he wanted from a woman was a single night of strictly physical passion, he had certainly come to the wrong address. As she opened her mouth, intending to tell him that, he suddenly moved toward her, bent his head and gave her a light yet somehow promising kiss, warm lips coaxing hers apart for too brief an instant.

"I'll go now and let you think it over—until Sunday," he announced, rising to his feet to tower over her. He smiled. "I forgot to mention I've been asked to talk to a group of psychology majors at the university Sunday afternoon. They want me to discuss my objections to programs like yours. I told Dr. Withers, head of the department, that the topic would be more interesting if you were there to give your point of view too. He agreed. I hope you don't already have plans?"

"Well, no, but I—"

"We can go together, then. I'll pick you up about one-twenty."

"But—"

"You do want the chance to respond to my objections, don't you?"

"Yes, of course, but . . . maybe I shouldn't go to the university with you," she suggested, moving forward to sit on the edge of the cushion while he picked up his coat, put it on and folded his tie into his pocket. "After all, we're on opposite sides and it might look funny for us to show up there together."

"I don't think anybody'll notice," he said wryly. "Our little controversy probably won't ever be reported on network news, so I doubt we'll set any tongues wagging by going to the university together."

"Maybe you're right," she conceded, and when he started across the room toward the door, she called after him, "Jim . . . about tonight . . . I didn't mean to lead you on. I want us to just be friends."

Turning back to her, he allowed his gaze to wander slowly from the tips of her toes to the top of her head. He shook his head. "Ashley, we'll never be just friends. Friends and lovers, yes, but not just friends. We're going to have something very special together."

"You—can't be so sure of that."

"Oh, but I am. Some things are inevitable."

Her answering sigh was a mingling of exasperation and bewilderment. "Jim, this is crazy. There must be lots of women in your life who'd love to be involved with you."

"There might be a few. But you're different, Ashley. It's you I'm interested in. I'll be here Sunday about one-twenty," he said, and without another word he opened the door and walked out.

Touching her fingertips to her lips, Ashley was lost

for a moment in the memory of his kisses. Then she shook her head. Although he was attractive and extremely persuasive, she would resist him. She truly was content with her life the way it was, and she wasn't going to let him complicate it.

CHAPTER FOUR

Sunday's debate before the psychology scholars produced some heated exchanges between Ashley and Jim. College students are notoriously tough questioners, and nearly every inquiry tossed at the debaters provoked a civilized argument, accentuating their difference of opinion and widening the gap between them, or so it seemed to Ashley. Although Jim had expressed a personal interest in her only two days ago, he attacked her position regarding call-in radio shows with no holds barred, employing practically every tactic in the book except resorting to scurrilous name-calling to convince the audience he was right. And Ashley responded in kind, answering his rhetoric with a keen and often biting defense. Their appearance together on Fred Naylor's television show had been a love-in compared to this encounter, and by the time it ended after an hour and a half, Ashley was unusually warm and she longed to shed her suit jacket.

After Dr. Withers made some closing comments and the students got up from their seats to mill around the lecture hall, Ashley picked up her purse and stepped from the speaker's platform. A hand descended on her shoulder and she glanced around, pressing her lips tightly together as Jim followed her down the two steps.

"Well, you certainly came out fighting today," she

said angrily. "Don't you think you went a bit far when you suggested people who do programs like mine are becoming radio's answer to lonely hearts columnists? That was unfair and you know it. People don't just call me to discuss their love lives. Way over half my callers have altogether different kinds of problems. You gave these students the wrong impression—about my show, anyhow. Next time stick to the facts."

"I have my facts straight about radio call-in shows in general," he responded matter-of-factly. "And I admitted yours is better than most."

"Thanks very much for another back-handed compliment. I'll cherish it forever," she said flippantly, then heaved a sigh. "Look, I know we aren't ever going to agree about this, but I think you can at least be fair."

"Was it fair of you to suggest I'm an elitist?" he countered. "You insinuated I think everyone with a problem should see a psychiatrist, and I don't think anything of the sort."

"Sometimes you give that impression and I—" She stopped short, detecting the sudden glint of amusement in his eyes. "You're enjoying this, aren't you?"

"I'm enjoying you. I like a woman with spirit and a mind of her own. And you have both, so how can I resist you?"

"For heaven's sake, will you be serious?"

"I am being very serious," he declared softly. "You just don't believe me—yet."

She searched her brain for a snappy answer but none was forthcoming. He was being deliberately provocative, and she wasn't prepared to deal with him in that kind of mood at that moment. Students were everywhere, one group standing only a couple feet away, and it simply wasn't the time or place to try to conduct a personal conversation. She eyed him warily when he moved closer and lowered his head to whisper, "But you will soon."

"Will what soon?"

"Believe I can't resist you."

"I never realized until this minute that you're a flirt," she murmured accusingly, but couldn't fight back a small smile. "Now that I know you are, maybe I shouldn't believe anything you—"

"Well, now, you two certainly gave my students something to think about," Dr. Withers inadvertently interrupted as he joined them at the platform. He nodded approval. "It's always stimulating to hear both sides of an issue presented so strongly. Dr. Miller, I have to admit that before today I tended to agree with Jim about radio psychologists, but you made so many good points that I may have to reconsider."

"I hope you will. And call me Ashley, please."

"Ashley it is," Withers agreed, eyeing her speculatively. "You're Tom Miller's daughter, aren't you? He's a fine man. You didn't get your doctorate in psychology here—I'd remember if you did. Where did you go to school?"

"Denver. Thought I'd try life away from my own hometown for a while without having to go too far away. Denver was the perfect place, and I loved it there."

"I'm sure your father's pleased you came back here to join his—" Dr. Withers's words halted when he saw someone frantically beckoning him across the lecture hall. He plowed his fingers through his hair. "Ashley, Jim, would you excuse me? I'd better go see what's happening over there."

They nodded, and as he hurried away, they were approached by an auburn-haired male student who ambled over, his hands in his pockets. He introduced himself. "Dr. Miller, Dr. Saxon, I'm Craig Norman." He turned his full attention to Ashley, and for several seconds his lips twitched as if he were about to smile. Instead his expression grew increasingly troubled, almost anguished, and he announced brokenly, "I k-keep hearing . . . voices . . . in my head. Th-they're telling me to do things I don't w-want to do!"

The voice-hearer in person! Recognizing the speech instantly, she nearly laughed but instead forced herself to glower at the young man. "So you're the one?" she said. "I suppose you think what you did was hilarious?"

"Well, uh, I . . ." Craig mumbled, looking around quickly at a friend who was hovering in the background. "I . . ."

"Didn't I tell you you'd better keep your big mouth shut?" the friend asked, stepping forward. He smiled weakly at Ashley and Jim. "I told him you wouldn't be glad to meet him. But he just had to come over and—"

"I thought I'd better apologize," Craig hastily put in, producing a smile that was more a wince. "I just wanted to win the bet. That's the only reason I did it. You see, all the guys were so sure I couldn't trick—er, make you believe I was ready for the loony bin."

"If you're really taking a psychology course, you must know that 'ready for the loony bin' is *not* the way we properly describe disturbed people," Ashley said stiffly. "Is it, Mr. Norman?"

"No. Oh, no, and I didn't mean to say it like that." He hunched his shoulders. "Sorry."

Unable to keep up the pretense any longer, Ashley dropped her stony mask and shrugged agreeably. "All right, apology accepted. You're forgiven. But don't pull any more stunts like that, okay?"

Craig released an audible sigh of relief, relaxed, and nodded. "It'll never happen again, I promise."

"Fine. Now, I think you owe Dr. Saxon an apology too for the time he wasted because of you."

"Sure. Sorry, Dr. Saxon," Craig said, thrusting his hand out to Jim. "But I never imagined Dr. Miller would call in a psychiatrist. And after what you said about programs like hers today, I'm kind of surprised you were willing to be at the station to talk to me that last time I called in."

Releasing the younger man's hand, Jim smiled and looked at Ashley. "I was there because Dr. Miller's a very persuasive woman."

"I'll say she is," Craig's friend spoke up. "Excuse me for saying so, Dr. Saxon, but I think you're wrong about her show. I never miss it."

"Because it's entertaining or because it's informative?"

"Both."

Nodding agreement, Craig smiled somewhat sheepishly at Ashley. "Well, I'm glad you're not mad. Guess we better get going."

"You're a freshman, aren't you, Craig?" she asked before the boys turned to leave. He nodded. "Decided yet what your major's going to be?"

"I've been thinking about computer sciences."

"Think about drama, too, while you're at it," she suggested wryly. "Judging from the performance you gave on the phone, you might have a future in the theater."

Grinning broadly, Craig gave his friend a poke in the ribs with his elbow as the two of them walked away.

For nearly a half hour students wandered over to talk to Ashley and Jim. After the last few drifted away and the lecture hall was almost empty, Jim escorted Ashley up the aisle toward the exit. "We can go now. Dr. Withers is obviously tied up; I'll talk to him later."

"Speaking of Dr. Withers, I have to admit I feel like I've scored a minor victory just by convincing him to reconsider the value of programs like mine," she said, glancing sideways at Jim. "And although I didn't keep count, I think it's obvious more of the students we talked to agree with me than with you."

"Gloating doesn't become you. Don't be smug."

"Who? Me?" she asked innocently.

"Three fourths of the people in the world might agree on something, but that doesn't necessarily make it right, does it?"

"Now, wait just a damned minute. I was only kidding about Dr. Withers and the students agreeing with me," Ashley muttered indignantly, stopping dead at the outside doors to glare up at him. "But if you want to start the debate all over again, I'll—"

"Whoa. Peace," he commanded quietly, placing a silencing finger against her lips. "There's no use in us talking about this because we just go around in circles, so let's declare another truce. Okay?"

He was right. It was useless to argue. So she nodded as they stepped outside the building together and were buffeted by the whipping wind. They ran across the parking lot to his car. It was good to get inside and settle into the front passenger seat, but her teeth were still chattering a little when he slipped in beneath the steering wheel. Wasting no time, he turned the key in the ignition and started the heater. Ashley was already warming up by the time they left the campus.

Jim turned south on Highway 72, announcing, "I thought we could go to my house for a while."

"Not today," she said. Being alone with him in his home in those secluded woods seemed to her like a dangerous chance to take. He could be too persuasive, and she knew only too well how attracted she was to him.

She shook her head. "I should go straight home; I have a lot of things I need to do."

"Those things can wait. I can't. You have to go home with me," he insisted, steering easily with one hand on the wheel, his other arm around her shoulder. He gave her a mysterious smile before turning his attention back to the road. "I have a surprise for you."

"A surprise? What kind?"

"I've said all I'm going to say about it."

"But—"

"My lips are sealed."

"I don't have any idea what it could be."

"That's right," he agreed, his tone teasing. "That's why it's going to be a surprise."

Tapping her toes against the floorboard, she looked out her window, racking her brain trying to imagine what the surprise might be, but she couldn't even come up with any possibilities. After several minutes she could stand the suspense no longer and, turning sideways in her seat, touched Jim's arm. "Come on, be fair. At least give me a hint or two."

Laughing softly, he looked at her. "You sound like a kid before Christmas, trying to guess what's in the boxes under the tree. You even have the same glow of excitement in your eyes. I guess I could give you one little hint."

"Yes," she said, nodding her head eagerly.

But then he shook his. "Naw, I don't think I will."

"Devil," she called him, swatting his arm yet smiling despite herself as she relaxed once more. "I'm not going to beg you to tell me what the surprise is. I'm just going to forget about it."

"Good idea," he murmured, then added mischievously, "but I know you're going to like it."

She poked the tip of her tongue out at him, then

joined in his answering laughter. It was good to be with him. Playful or serious, he was an intriguing companion. Even when they argued, she felt he truly listened to what she said and respected her right to have an opinion different from his. During today's debate she had thought he had gone a little too far with some of his remarks, but then she probably had, too, in the heat of the moment.

They didn't argue as they headed on toward his house. Following the twisting stretch of road, they simply talked about this and that, anything that came to mind. And Ashley enjoyed the scenery, as she always did in this area. In pale sunlight, fallen gold aspen leaves carpeted patches of ground beneath stark bare trees. Occasionally she caught glances of silvery streams through the forests.

"It's beautiful here," she murmured. "I used to like to come up this way when there was snow on the ground."

"The first snow we have, I'll bring you up and take you for a drive in the Jeep on the back road that's behind my house. The ride won't be smooth, but the scenery's terrific. Rolling meadowland on both sides of the road. I'm sure you'll love it."

"It does sound like a lovely place," she replied noncommittally, wondering if he would remember to reissue his invitation when the first snow actually fell.

Meeting a white pickup truck on the road, Jim waved at the driver and passenger, who both waved back. "Jack and Rosie Franklin, my nearest neighbors," he explained to Ashley. "They live just over the hill from me, but I can't see their place from mine."

"Don't you ever get a little lonely way out here?" she asked, observing him closely, her gaze exploring the clean-cut line of his profile. "I mean, it's so isolated. I've thought a lot about getting a place far away from town but wonder if I should. Privacy is very important to me, but maybe it could be too much of a good thing, like anything else. Are there times, especially in winter, when you feel a little stir-crazy and wish more people were close by?"

"There are times when I'd like to have someone with me," he answered somewhat evasively, slowing to turn onto his winding drive. Glancing at her, he gave her a slow, lazy smile. "But no, I don't wish I had close neighbors all around me. I was brought up on a ranch, though, so I'm used to a certain amount of isolation."

"And I was raised in a nice suburban neighborhood, other houses all around."

"But you did say you're the kind of person who needs time alone," Jim reminded her softly. "That was one of the reasons you don't want to get involved with anyone, isn't it? Because you don't have enough time to yourself as it is?"

"Oh, the holly bushes in front of your house are beautiful," she said, swiftly changing the subject as they approached the stone-and-cedar structure. "I didn't notice them the other night when I was here. Too dark, I guess."

"I guess," he repeated wryly, and his indulgent expression indicated quite clearly that her ploy hadn't gone unnoticed. Yet he didn't press the issue and said nothing more until after he'd stopped the car and they'd got out and gone into the house. He took her into the great room.

"I'll start a fire," he said, motioning her to the sofa while shedding his brown tweed jacket. "Have a seat. Relax. I'll have a blaze going in no time."

Resting against the comfortable cushion, she watched him kneel on the hearth and begin to break kindling into smaller pieces to place on the grate. The muscles of his shoulders rippled under his tan sweater as he leaned forward, and the virile lineation of his thighs was briefly defined when he rose with athletic ease to his feet and bent to gather three nice-size logs from the wrought-iron rack next to the fireplace. He placed them atop the kindling, then kneeled again to strike a match and hold the flame to the stripped bark until it caught. When he sat back on his heels, the ends of his thick, sandy hair nearly touched his shirt collar in back, and her heart gave a silly little lurch. For a wild, crazy instant she ached to run her fingers through the crisp strands but she mustered the will to suppress that insanely intense need when he stood and turned toward her. She managed a nonchalant smile.

Dusting his hands off, he asked, "Care for a brandy?"

She tilted her head to one side questioningly. "Is that the surprise?"

"I knew you hadn't forgotten," he said, amusement in his eyes. "No, that isn't the surprise. But since you can't seem to wait any longer, I'll show you what it is. But first you have to close your eyes." She complied and he added, "Now keep them shut until I get back from the kitchen."

"The surprise is food?"

"Stop guessing," he admonished, his voice fading as he strode away. "It isn't anything you can possibly be imagining. Be right back."

Willing to play the game, Ashley sat relaxed on the sofa, her hands loosely clasped in her lap, her eyes squeezed shut. She heard Jim's quiet footsteps on the hardwood floor less than a minute later, then felt the cuff of one trouser leg brush her ankle when he stepped in front of her.

"Okay," he said a couple of seconds later. "You can open them now."

She did, looking up at his lean, tanned face at first until he glanced down and she did also, finding at her feet a cardboard box containing four fuzzy, active black kittens with white markings tumbling all over one another. Immediately she was on her knees on the rug, peering into the box. "Oh, Jim, they're pretty," she softly exclaimed. "But you never mentioned you had a cat."

"I don't. These belong to friends who had to go out of town for the weekend. I'm baby-sitting."

"But where's their mother?"

"In the kitchen. I think she decided it was the perfect time to have a meal in peace."

Unable to resist, Ashley picked up a kitten. "Do you think she'll mind?"

"I doubt it," Jim said. "Mama seems to be getting a little impatient with her brood."

"This *is* a complete surprise," Ashley admitted, picking up the rest of the kittens one at a time, then pushing aside the box. She looked up at him. "I never expected this."

He looked down at her. "I know. And I have to tell you the truth. I volunteered to baby-sit this weekend because I wanted to make a good impression by showing you I was willing to take care of a mama cat and her kittens."

She laughed. "I don't believe that for a minute. You just love animals too."

"Well, maybe that has a little something to do with it," he conceded, grinning. "But mainly I did this to impress you."

"That sounds like a line to me, Dr. Saxon," she said

blithely. "I've heard a few in my time, but I have to warn you I'm never gullible enough to believe them."

She gave him a cheeky grin, and he watched her focus her attention on the irrepressible kittens gamboling around her, playing half hearted games of tag, wriggling onto their backs to paw the air, and chewing each other's ears. Sunlight streaming through the windows opposite the couch caught in Ashley's golden hair, casting it in a silver shimmer, and when she gently lifted one white-pawed kitten and touched its bewhiskered face to her cheek, his features gentled without her noticing. He stepped away from her. "Excuse me a minute. I'll be right back."

"Okay." She nodded, then laughed softly when two of the kittens playfully tangled and did a perfect somersault together. It was a minute or two later when she heard a distinct click and saw a bright flash of light out of the corner of her eye. She jerked her head around to find Jim standing on the other side of the coffee table, camera in hand. She grimaced. "What are you doing?"

"Photography's one of my hobbies," he told her, taking two steps to the left to alter the camera angle. "You and the kittens are perfect subjects."

"Oh no, not me," she objected strenuously, turning her head away. "Maybe it's silly, but I don't feel comfortable having my picture taken."

"Just relax. Play with the kittens," he coaxed. "Forget I have a camera."

And after a while she did. The kittens, endearing and so cute, nearly hypnotized her with their comic antics, and she scarcely noticed the clicking camera and the accompanying flash until almost fifteen minutes later, when the kittens started to tire and open their mouths in huge yawns, exposing needle-sharp little teeth and pink tongues. As their mother loped gracefully out of the kitchen, they gathered around her, mewing hungrily. Gently picking up Mama Cat, Ashley put her in the box and one by one returned her babies to her, smiling as they eagerly nuzzled up to her belly.

Jim put down the camera and carried the box back to the kitchen. While he was gone, Ashley got off her knees, brushed off her skirt and wandered across the room to the French doors that opened to the terrace. The wind chased leaves across the flagstone, and the towering trees beyond swayed together. For a minute or two she watched the tops of the pines bowing like graceful dancers, and when Jim returned and joined her at the door, she turned to him, smiling.

"The kittens were really a nice surprise. Thank you for letting me play with them."

"I mentioned you to my friends, and they wanted me to be sure to tell you that the kittens are up for adoption," he said. "How about it? Would you like to have one of them when they're weaned?"

"Oh, don't tempt me," she said with a groan. "I'd love to have one, but Ludlow would never stand for the competition. He hates for other cats even to come into my yard. A kitten wouldn't have a chance around him."

"He doesn't want to share you, hmmm?"

"That's putting it mildly. That cat thinks he owns me."

Smiling softly, Jim touched her hair, rubbing a silken strand between thumb and forefinger as he murmured, "I can't really blame him for being possessive where you're concerned. Just shows what good taste he has."

"Tell me, is photography really one of your hobbies?" Ashley hastily asked, stepping past him to view the collection of pictures mounted on the side wall. "Did you take all these?"

"As a matter of fact, I did," he answered, a hint of

amusement in his voice. "Most of these were taken in the last year or so."

"They're very good. I especially like the one of the mountain lake. The reflection of the trees on the water —beautiful," she said sincerely, impressed by his talent. "Do you have more I can see?"

"Come with me," he said, his hand lightly touching the small of her back while he guided her upstairs along the hall where more photos were hanging. He pointed out three taken on his family's ranch and named some of the landmarks. "That's Little Mesa. And this is Lonesome Pine Creek."

"Did you go wading there when you were a kid?"

"Whenever I could sneak away from my chores." Jim smiled reminiscently. "On a ranch everyone has to work hard, and sometimes Evelyn, Mark and I just wanted to goof off. Mark generally got caught in the barn behind bales of hay, reading a comic book."

"Ah, sounds like you were three very normal kids," Ashley remarked, moving farther down the hall. "And speaking of kids, who are the two in this picture?"

"My niece and nephew. Evelyn's children. I took that this summer when they were down here from Oregon."

Ashley inspected one of the toddlers more closely, then looked hard at Jim. "Uh-huh, your nephew does resemble you a little bit. It's the eyes mainly, and the shape of the mouth."

"I always knew he was a great-looking kid," said Jim, his expression deadpan. "Now I know why."

"I'm sure Evelyn and her husband deserve some of the credit too," she retorted, grinning as she stepped in front of the last photograph on the wall. A black and white, it was of a huge full moon rising just above the tops of tall pine trees. Somehow it was serene and exciting at the same time. She nodded approval. "Oh, I really like this. I like them all."

"You haven't seen them all. There are more in here," he said, catching her hand in his to take her into his bedroom.

At first sight she liked the room with its own stone fireplace and cleanly designed pecan furniture. Carpeted in red, it had two large windows with tan pinch-pleated drapes, and the coverlet on the bed was a smart-looking design of red, tan and black contemporary stripes on a beige background. It looked like a man's room, devoid of frills, and it suited Jim. There were the usual little personal touches here and there, including the photographs on the right wall, which she walked over to see. They were some of his best, and she couldn't decide which was her favorite—the one of a single juniper standing tall in a lush meadow or the one of two women sitting on a cabin porch shelling green peas into white enamel pans.

"All your pictures are so peaceful," she commented softly after a minute. "They make me feel quiet."

"That's the kind I want to take. After spending most of my time trying to help people deal with their problems, I look for whatever's peaceful and quiet."

"To relieve some of the stress," she murmured understandingly. His work was even more stressful than her own, because he saw more severely disturbed patients. He coped with it well, though. In his private life he relaxed and found laughter and had hobbies like photography to help ease tension. Tapping her right forefinger against her jaw, she studied both her favorite pictures once more, then reached a decision. "I think the women shelling peas is my favorite one of all."

"It's yours, then," he offered, standing behind her. "You can take it home."

"Oh no, I wasn't hinting."

"I know you weren't. Since you like it, I want you to have it," he insisted, his hands encircling her waist.

At his touch, she tensed, her heart leaping. When he drew her back against the hard, lithe length of his body, she started to protest, but the words died in her throat as he bent to trace tender nibbling kisses along the side of her neck, setting wildfires on the surface of her skin. She suppressed a pleasured moan. His hand left her waist and skimmed lightly over her breasts. She shook her head. "Jim, no."

"Oh yes," he nearly growled, turning her toward him, tangling his fingers in her hair, the heels of his hands tilting her face up as his descended.

His dark eyes filled her vision and her eyes fluttered shut the instant his warm lips softly touched her own. And when his arms swept around her, she was suddenly glad because she realized she cared for him . . . very much. He made her feel happy, gloriously alive and delighted by her own femininity. She moved closer to him, needing to feel more fully the latent power of his male body. She slipped her arms upward, curving them around his shoulders, and as his mouth hardened to take sure, swift possession of hers, she relaxed in his tightening embrace, the tip of her tongue parrying the gently invasive push of his.

"Oh, yes, this is better. I've been wanting to do this all afternoon," he whispered in her ear long moments later. "You're lucky I didn't grab you while we were still in the lecture hall. I wanted to."

"You're crazy."

"No. Perfectly sane. A man who *didn't* want you would have to be crazy," he uttered roughly, deftly removing her suit jacket, then undoing the small bow of her blouse. He unfastened the first two buttons, pulled the fine georgette fabric aside and forged a chain of searing kisses over satiny skin on her collarbone. "And I want you like hell, so you don't have to worry about my sanity."

"But—"

"Come here," he demanded urgently, taking a backward step toward the easy chair nearby. He sat, smoldering coals of desire lighting his dark eyes as he drew her between his legs, then down into his waiting arms again. Burying his face in her hair, he whispered her name as she lifted a hand to caress his face, her slender fingers unsteady and light as a breeze upon his cheeks. With a fingertip he outlined the inviting bow shape of her lips, then followed the natural arch of her eyebrows and feathered the very tips of her long, thick lashes. His gaze imprisoned hers. "You have such compelling eyes," he whispered.

Mesmerized by word and touch, hypnotized by the raw virility that emanated from him, she murmured, "So do you."

"And your skin's like warm satin."

"Yours . . . I like touching you."

"God, I can't keep my hands off you," he muttered, his voice endearingly uneven as he wrapped her in his arms and his lips descended with persuasive power onto hers once more. Unhurried, patient, he held her close, plying her with deep-searching kisses while his hands lightly roamed, barely grazing her calves, the length of her thighs, her curving waist and round, firm breasts.

Breathing raggedly, feeling the fast, steady beat of his heart against her, she was swept up in a heady whirlwind of rising passion. She eased her hands beneath his sweater, tugged his shirttail free of the waistband of his trousers, and eagerly sought the feel of his bare, heated flesh. With her fingers she shaped the strong, ridged column of his spine, feeling muscles flex beneath her caresses. Delighting in her ability to arouse him, she ran her nails lightly over his lean sides, smiling secretly against his lips when he groaned softly in response.

With probing tongue, he plundered the honeyed sweetness of her mouth, desire stirring to a nearly intolerable frenzy in him. Molten fire seemed to be surging through his veins, gathering in pulsing pressure in his loins. He needed her, ached for her, wanted to possess her completely.

Yet despite the passion she sensed simmering hotly just beneath the surface in him, he was incredibly gentle. She was hopelessly lost in her growing affection for him and near-primitive sexual longing. She cared about him, and he seemed to care about her. Right now that was enough to loosen the rein on her inhibitions. Unable to think, she could only feel while his marauding lips played with hers and she gave him back kiss for kiss. Her fingertips inched over his flat nipples in their nests of fine hair. She felt the shudder that ran through him.

"Ashley, you're driving me crazy," he whispered, his warm breath tickling her ear as he crushed her against him. "I may not be able to let you go now."

"Don't," she whispered back. "Kiss me again."

"Yes, love, I plan to. Again and again." Keeping that promise, he undid the rest of her blouse. Moving her this way and that, he stripped the blouse off and allowed it to slip from his fingers to drift down onto the floor at his feet. He pressed her down upon his lap. His glinting black eyes held her as he eased his fingers beneath the straps of both her slip and bra, drawing them aside until they fell around her upper arms. His gaze sought the exposed shadowed valley between her breasts and he leaned forward to place his lips against the beginning swells of sweet feminine flesh. Then, cradling her in his arms, he stood up. "Let's go to bed, Ashley," he whispered, kissing her again as he carried her across the room and put her down on the coverlet. Sitting beside her, he stripped off his sweater and lifted her hands to his shirt front, conveying with a glance instead of words what he wanted. A slow smile touched his mouth when she began undoing the buttons.

His skin was bronze-toned and like velvet-sheathed steel, smooth and warm to the touch yet underlaid with solid sinew and muscle. Her fingers floated along his arms from wrists to broad shoulders, then down over his chest, her nails tugging lightly at fine dark-brown hair.

He came down above her, gently clasping her face in strong, capable hands as he kissed her once, twice, many times, his lips applying a tender, twisting pressure. Leisurely he explored her slender, shapely body.

And as she kissed him in return with near abandon, her hands stroked his back. Hot all over, aching deep inside, she was almost lost in the passion he evoked in her and glad when he lowered the top of her slip to her waist and unfastened her bra to bare her breasts. Her breath came in shallow, rapid sweeps as he looked down at the swift rise and fall of the firmly rounded mounds of flesh.

"You're so beautiful," he whispered, and she softly gasped as he touched her then, his lean fingertips roaming freely over satiny skin before playing over and around erect, peach-tinted nipples.

"Jim," she murmured huskily when he lowered his head. And she swept her fingers through his sandy hair, moaning softly as his mouth closed around the throbbing peak of her left breast. With his tongue, he toyed with the topmost nubble of flesh, and wild sensations, like electrical charges, surged through her, scorching every nerve ending. He was making her want him too much, and suddenly all her misgivings came rushing back. Something deep within her, something her body cursed, made her stiffen, unable to seek the ultimate delight she knew instinctively she could share with this special man. Caution stronger than desire held her back, and she moved restlessly, shaking her head.

"Jim, I—hell, I just can't."

"Ashley, you . . ." he began, raising himself slightly to look down at her, his jaw clenched. His eyes impaled hers. "What if I won't let you go now?"

"You will," she murmured, wanting to touch his face but not allowing herself to do that. "You're an honorable person; you'll let me go just because I want you to."

"Why the devil did you have to say that?" he said with a groan. "How can I possibly do anything dishonorable now?"

"I don't expect you to."

"Do you know what you're doing to me?" he asked, his voice raspy. "I know you're not a woman who can be rushed, but many more episodes like this and I . . . I want you and you want me too; I can tell. But you keep fighting me."

"I told you I don't want to get in—"

"Involved. I know what you said. You'd better get dressed," he muttered, rising to his feet and getting off the bed, picking up his shirt and sweater and leaving the room without looking back.

Chewing her lower lip, Ashley got up too.

Forty minutes later, at Ashley's house, Jim walked her to the front door and waited until she unlocked it to take her by the shoulders and turn her toward him. "I'm flying to California in the morning. I've been invited to be on a couple of talk shows, but I'll only be gone a few days."

"Oh. And are you going on the shows to voice your objections to radio psychologists?"

He nodded. "But I'll be appearing on both with someone who agrees with you on the issue."

"Maybe he'll have better luck getting you to change your mind than I've had."

"I doubt it very much. If you can't persuade me, nobody can," he said, half smiling as he touched a tendril of her hair. "I'll be back Wednesday. See you then."

"Maybe . . . Maybe we shouldn't see each other so much."

"You're fighting me again," he accused. "But I'm not going to give up. We want each other. That's it."

His confidence unnerved her a little, but she didn't show it and shook her head. "Listen, Jim—"

"Wednesday. I'll be in touch," he said, giving her a quick kiss before opening the door, then nodding good night when she stepped inside the house. She closed the door behind her, and he walked back to his car, a thoughtful frown knitting his brow. He had told her the truth. He did want her and didn't intend to let their relationship end the way she said she wanted it to—without any real involvement whatsoever.

CHAPTER FIVE

Ashley was in the kitchen Wednesday evening when she heard a knock at her front door. Her heart jumped with excitement she tried to control. It might not be Jim who was knocking. But she hoped . . . Quickly crossing the living room, she parted the draperies just enough to peer out the window and smiled when she saw Jim's car parked in her driveway. She wasted no time opening the door.

Jim stood on the porch, his hands thrust in his trouser pockets, his shoulders slightly hunched. His eyes met hers as he softly said, "Hello. Told you I'd be in touch."

"Yes, well, come in where it's warm," she said. "When did you get back?"

"About an hour ago, after two flight delays," he said, stepping into the house, then closing the door for her. "I would have been here sooner but the traffic from the airport was really heavy."

The curve of her brow lifted. "You haven't been home yet?"

"I wanted to see you first."

"Had dinner?"

"On the plane."

"Would you like some coffee? I could—"

"Maybe later. First things first," he murmured, tilting her chin up to give her a brief but incredibly thorough kiss. Then he allowed his gaze to wander slowly over her, nodding his approval of the jewel-bright blue caftan she wore. "That matches the color of your eyes exactly. I like it. You look lovely."

"Thank you," she replied politely, keeping secret the fact that she had picked the caftan for that very reason and had also taken extra care with her makeup and hair just because she knew he might drop by tonight. There was no reason to let him know she wanted to look especially nice for him; he was self-confident enough already. She motioned him to the sofa. "Let's sit down. Tell me about the TV shows you did."

"First you tell me if you missed me," he countered, settling down beside her. "Did you?"

She managed a light shrug. "Well, it's been a very busy three days."

"I didn't ask if you'd been busy," he reminded her, his slow grin playful, almost boyish. "I asked if you missed me."

"How could I when just last night I saw you on the Callahan show?" was her evasive answer. "When did you go to Denver to tape that one?"

"Ummm, about a week ago."

"You're taking your crusade everywhere, aren't you? Out of town, out of state," she murmured, her expression growing rather troubled. "I understand you have reservations about radio psychologists because of what happened to your patient, but maybe you're letting your opposition to them consume too much of your time."

"I don't think so."

"But what about your patients? Their sessions with you are very important to them, and you've been away three days this week."

"And I'll see them all before the end of the week. I've

rearranged my schedule, and I'll be in my office on Saturday. I'm not neglecting any of them."

"But how long can you go on that way, pushing yourself, trying to do everything?" she protested softly, concern in her eyes. "Being a psychiatrist is stressful enough. Why add the role of crusader?"

"Ah, you're worried about me," he said teasingly. "That's sweet."

"Don't make jokes," she chided, scowling. "I'm being serious."

His expression sobered. "Making jokes is one of the ways I deal with the pressures."

"I know it is, but right now I really want to talk about this."

"All right. I do what I'm doing because I feel I have to. It's as simple as that," he stated. "Ashley, if all radio call-in shows were like yours, I'd just voice my reservations and let it go at that. But they're not. A few of these pop psychologists don't seem to give a damn what they say to their callers as long as it sounds like a good answer. For instance, in L.A. I listened to a program, 'Calling Dr. Merv Wheeler,' and heard him advise a caller who was obviously traumatized because her husband had left her and their three small children to load the kids off somewhere, take a vacation and find herself. As if it were that simple. How could he tell a woman in a state of depression to find herself? And most of the so-called answers he gave other callers were as superficial, although he does have a talent for making himself sound like he knows exactly what he's talking about. Which makes him even more dangerous."

Ashley winced. "This Merv Wheeler does sound irresponsible, but that doesn't mean all call-in hosts are."

"If only a few of them are, that's too many."

"I can agree with that, but . . ." She moved her

hands in an uncertain gesture. "But you must know you can't stop such shows from being on the air, because they're popular and stations make profits on them."

"I don't expect to be able to stop them, but I can expose them to the public for what they are—a new form of entertainment that shouldn't be taken seriously."

"I'm not in the entertainment business," she stated firmly. "And I don't want to be included in the same category as psychologists like Merv Wheeler. When you use words like 'expose to the public,' you make it sound like I'm involved in something criminal."

"Ashley," he murmured, holding her gaze. "I'm not attacking you personally."

She sighed. Maybe he wasn't, but sometimes it sure seemed that way. And whenever they talked about this, it always ended in a stalemate. This time was no exception. Realizing the discussion was going nowhere fast, as usual, she got up. "How about that coffee now?"

"Okay," he agreed amicably, then tagged along when she went into the kitchen.

Ten minutes later, back in the living room, Jim suddenly snapped his fingers and set his cup and saucer down on the table at the end of the sofa. "I almost forgot. I brought you a present," he announced, reaching into the inside pocket of his suit jacket and bringing out a huge chocolate bar, which he presented with a flourish and a low bow. "Enjoy it."

Laughing, she shook her head. "You shouldn't have. Really, you shouldn't have. I told you I can't resist chocolate, and I've never seen a candy bar this big. You know, don't you, that I'll eat every bite of it and then probably curse you the next time I get on the bathroom scale."

"I knew I'd be taking that chance," he admitted.

"But when I saw it in the airport gift shop, I knew it was just made for you. I had to buy it."

"And I'll have to eat it. I won't be able to stop myself," she said dryly, a teasing sparkle appearing in her eyes. "It's all your fault. You knew I wouldn't be able to resist temptation."

"And I'm hoping this isn't the only temptation you won't be able to resist tonight," he murmured, taking the chocolate bar out of her hand to put it aside. Gliding his fingers through her hair, cupping her face in his palms, he smiled gently and eased the edge of one thumb slowly back and forth across her lips. "While I was gone, I actually dreamed about touching you like this. And kissing you. And—"

"Jim, I—"

"Don't talk," he commanded softly. "I want you to kiss me, Ashley."

And she did, coaxed by his resonant voice and mesmerized by his dark eyes. Curving her hands across his shoulders, she leaned forward. Her eyes fluttered shut as her mouth sought his. Then she was in his arms and her arms were around him and her heart raced. Erotic sensations, wild and untrammeled, rushed through her, and her lips parted to the sweet, subtle mastery of his. As he gathered her closer, she willingly went, wanting the firm pressure of his body hard against her. Relaxing in his embrace, she opened her mouth to his plying kisses, the tip of her tongue boldly feathering his.

"Yes," he murmured roughly, burying his face in her hair for an instant before plundering her sweet, soft lips again and again. Hot desire throbbed through him as they hungrily kissed. Responsive and pliant, her shapely, slender body moving sinuously beneath his roaming hands, she fueled the flames burning in him. Primitive desire made him want to possess her quickly and completely, yet he didn't give in to that urge because he wanted long hours with her. He wanted her to want him as much as he wanted her, wanted to arouse her passion to a fever pitch as she had his. Hands spanning her waist, his fingers kneading and caressing, he trailed slow, nibbling kisses down her neck and whispered, "You did miss me."

"I . . ." she began, then softly gasped when his lips found her frantic pulsebeat. "Maybe I did . . . a little."

"Say it. Did you miss me?"

"Yes," she confessed breathlessly. And she had. She had missed him more than just a little and certainly much more than she had expected to. Was she in love? If not, she was close, and she knew it. She hadn't wanted anything like this to happen to her but it had and . . . All thought ceased, and raw emotion filled her entire being when he whispered endearments in her ear. Trembling as his warm breath sent shiver after shiver down her spine, she ran her fingers feverishly through his hair. "Yes, yes, I missed you." She felt his lips form a smile.

Catching the tender morsel of one earlobe between his teeth, Jim gently nibbled at it as he swept one hand along her side over the folds of her caftan. "You feel so good. Do you have anything on under this?"

"Of course I do."

"Curses," he muttered, nuzzling her neck with his nose. "Foiled again."

When he lifted his head to look down at her, she grinned and shook her head. "You're a very complex man. One minute you're deadly serious and the next you're . . ."

"We're all complex," he said between light, quick

kisses. "But I don't want to discuss basic psychological theory. Right now I'm interested in you—just you."

She believed him. Gazing into his penetrating eyes, she saw everything she wanted in a man—intelligence, tenderness, passion and respect. In a flash she knew. She did love him. Did he love her, though? She knew instinctively that he cared, and for the moment that was enough. Surrendering to the precious magic of being in love and knowing she was, she cupped the back of his head in one hand and urged him closer, giving his own words back to him. "I want you to kiss me, Jim."

"My pleasure," he uttered gruffly, and his finely sculpted lips brushed against hers repeatedly, then hardened to take sure, swift possession of her mouth, tasting the sweetness within. As she drew his tongue farther in against hers, a shudder ran over him. He cupped her breasts in his hands, lightly squeezing resilient feminine flesh. He wanted more. He needed to see and touch bare skin, and when she eased his coat off his shoulders, he swiftly discarded it and lifted the hem of her caftan, pushing it up over her legs, past her thighs to her waist and higher, smiling sensuously when her eyes flickered open to meet his. "I have to touch you."

"I want to touch you, too," she admitted, her voice husky. She unbuttoned his shirt.

He pulled it off, his heart hammering when fingers scampered over his naked chest. Unable to wait any longer, he drew the sapphire blue caftan over her head and carelessly tossed it aside.

Ashley's lacy bra quickly joined the caftan on the floor, and she felt delightfully erotic as Jim's smoldering eyes explored her body. When his fingertips began inscribing concentric circles upward around her breasts, she caught her breath, feeling as if his touch was igniting rings of fire.

"You're so beautiful," he murmured as she caressed his arms, his shoulders, his back. With thumb and forefinger he spanned the peaks of her breasts, rubbing one passion-aroused tip, then the other. "I want to taste you here. And here." His hand, gently parting her thighs, brushed upward. "Everywhere."

She was lost. He had awakened a longing deep within her that intensified with every passing second. Love sang through her, bursting out, seeking release, and she wanted to give that love and all of herself completely to Jim. She sighed with pleasure as he grazed tantalizing kisses in the valley between her breasts. Yet when he cradled her in his arms and rose effortlessly to his feet, unbidden practicalities clamored in her head. Her heart lurched.

"I can't let you go now," he whispered against her right temple. "Where's your bedroom?"

She wanted to throw caution to the wind and simply direct him there. Yet . . . "I—I'm not prepared for this," she said softly instead, nestling her face against his neck. "Precaution-wise, I mean."

"I knew you probably wouldn't be," was his quiet answer. "So I'm prepared."

Leaning back in his arms, she looked up at him, her eyes opening wider. "You were *that* sure I'd say yes?"

A wry smile tugged upward at the corners of his mouth. "Honey, I wasn't sure about anything. But hope springs eternal, so the old saying goes."

An answering smile quivered on her lips. "You're . . . incorrigible. Did you know that?"

"Hush," he whispered, silencing her with a long, impassioned kiss before reluctantly releasing her lips to repeat, "where's your room?"

"Down . . . the hall. Left."

He carried her there, kicked the door shut behind

them and, after throwing back the covers on her bed, lowered her almost reverently to the mattress, then switched on the lamp atop the nightstand. In the soft glowing light, Ashley's skin shimmered opalescently. He rose up from one knee to stand and unbuckle his belt.

Ashley watched him undress, taking in the powerful lines of his long legs, lean hips, tapered waist and broad chest. He was so magnificently male, and she longed to feel his heated flesh again. When he came down beside her on the bed, she moved a hand over his side. But as she started to draw the sheet up over both of them, he tossed it back.

"No, I want to see every inch of you," he explained. "And I want to be looking into your eyes when we—"

"Jim," she breathed, stopping his evocative words with a kiss that lingered for long, hushed moments.

"We're going to do the most pleasurable things together," he promised, touching her face with supreme tenderness. His fingertips wandered slowly over her delicate features as though he were committing them to memory, tracing the shape of her mouth and her full lower lip, then following the sweep of her high cheekbones to her temples. He felt the movement of her lashes against his skin as he kissed her eyes closed. "Honey, I want you so much."

His deep-timbred voice and the words he spoke made her senses swim. Feeling light-headed and exquisitely alive, she touched his face, too, loving the texture of his skin and the precise line of his jaw that conveyed such strength. She drew her fingers across his lips, smiling sensuously as he gently captured one fingertip between his teeth. He smiled back and she kissed one tiny dimple, then the other, breathing in the compelling scent of his aftershave.

On his side, leaning on one elbow, he toyed with a tendril of her hair. "Feels like warm silk," he said softly. "Every time I look at you I want to run my fingers through it, to see it tousled a little."

"I like yours tousled too," she admitted, tugging a sandy lock, causing it to fall forward across his forehead. "There. Now you look sort of rakish."

"And you look beautiful. Are beautiful," he murmured, his gaze caressing the length of her body. His hand followed the same path his eyes had taken, brushing over her bare breasts, across her abdomen, down to her shapely, smooth thighs before skimming back upward again. He slipped his fingers beneath the waistband of her lace-edged panties and began to lower them. "Help me," he whispered, and when she raised her hips an inch or so, he pulled the panties down her long legs and completely off.

Naked, she felt vulnerable and very aroused at the same time. The endearing warmth and respect conveyed by his expression kept her from being self-conscious. All her former reservations had vanished, and it seemed so right to be with him like this, ready, eager to give her love. She looked at him, her eyes shining softly.

Jim trickled his fingertips across her midriff, finding a tiny mole near her ribcage. As he touched it, her muscles contracted and she took a quick breath. He cocked one eyebrow. "You're ticklish?"

"Oh no. No," she lied.

"I think you are, but I'll find out for sure later. Right now . . ." He didn't bother to finish his sentence. Instead he turned her toward him and initiated a series of kisses that lengthened and deepened and heightened mutual desire.

It was a time of discovery. In the lampglow they searched out each other's secrets. He found that her back was incredibly sensitive, especially where it arched into her waist. Even the lightest touch of his lips there never failed to induce a shiver of excitement. And she found that the playful raking of her nails across his shoulders had the same effect on him. Unrushed, they came closer together emotionally as well as physically. Ashley sensed passion simmering hotly just beneath the surface in him but also sensed that he was holding it in strict control. For caring enough to do that, she loved him all the more, which made her all the more responsive and giving.

He was enthralled by her. The satiny sheen of her skin and the pure alabaster smoothness of its surface fascinated him. He blazed a trail of nipping kisses over the curve of her buttocks, along the backs of her thighs and down the calves of her legs, past her ankles, all the way to the soles of her feet, lazily flicking the tip of his tongue against her arches. Squirming, she couldn't suppress a giggle.

He smiled. "Ah, so you are ticklish. I knew it. You realize I can use that knowledge as a powerful weapon, don't you?"

"You wouldn't?" she gasped as his tongue skipped over her sole again. *"Would* you?"

"No, not at the moment anyway." Turning her over, he continued the trail of kisses upward, soon causing the muscles of her abdomen to flutter. Kneeling beside her, he cupped her breasts in his hands, his fingers pressing lightly down against her firm full flesh before etching feathery scrolls upon her taut hot skin. With his thumbs he drew rousing arcs over her roseate nipples and teased the inviting buds of flesh. His senses inflamed by her quiet moans of delight, he bent to swiftly take one succulent pinnacle into his mouth, pulling deeply at it, his lips, teeth and tongue almost devouring.

"Oh Jim," she softly cried, linking her fingers over his nape. An explosive force built to volcanic levels in the very center of her being, and all her nerve endings were set afire. At that moment he could have done anything he wanted with her and she would have gladly given; her love knew no boundaries. Her hands drifted from his shoulders down his arms to the hard plane of his back, moving tremulously. Adrift in spiraling passion, she felt his every touch as if it were a searing brand that would forever more remain scorched on her skin, burning through her flesh to the marrow of her bones. His mouth left her breasts and she felt bereft until he parted her legs, moved between them, and his questing lips descended on her own. Taking her small hand in his, he drew it downward between them and she curved her fingers around him.

"You're driving me crazy. If we're going to be careful, we'd better start now." He reached toward the nightstand and tucked the necessary sheath into her hand. "Do it for me, love."

Hesitantly, inexpertly, she did, but he didn't seem to mind her lack of expertise. His fingers grazed upward between her thighs, seeking her most exquisite warmth and gently charting secret feminine hills and vales.

Ashley felt faint. Sensations, primitive and blissful, claimed her, and inner emptiness became a yearning ache only Jim could fill. She moved sinuously with his caresses, wrapping her arms around him as he lowered himself down upon her. Yet as she felt the pulsating pressure of him stir against her, she involuntarily tensed.

"I need you, Ashley."

"I . . . need you . . . too. But I've . . ."

"Baby, try to relax," he coaxed, kissing the corners of her mouth. "I'm going to be very gentle with you, I promise." And with a tender thrust he entered her, his lips on hers capturing her first soft sound. He groaned as her heated body flowered open to receive him.

She pressed her nails down upon the flexed muscles beneath his shoulder blades as he filled her completely, partially assuaging the emptiness she had felt. And the genuine affection she saw tempering the passionate fire in his eyes as she gazed up at him brought her happiness more intense than she had ever experienced. Smiling tremulously, caught in profound emotion, she raised a hand to play idly with the lock of hair brushing his brow.

Still for a long moment, he looked down at her, enchanted by the faint glow that illuminated her features, by her sapphire eyes and by the small smile that lingered on her lips. Kissing her, he whispered, "Ashley, you feel so good."

"So do you," she whispered back.

"I may not let you get much sleep tonight."

"I don't think I'll mind at all," she confessed. And when he began to move unhurriedly within her, she moved with him, soon matching her rhythm to his and drifting upward in a realm of building sensations. On fire, breathing fast, she wrapped her arms and legs around him. He created flutterings light as butterfly wings inside her. The flutters came faster and faster, soon melding together in white-hot rapture. Spasms of pleasure rushed through her and she pulled closer to him as he stroked harder and more quickly.

"Ashley," he groaned.

"Oh Jim, yes. *Yes,*" she breathed. And then she was there, poised on the piercing spire of ecstasy, a sunburst of warmth exploding in her, making her cry out his name again. He joined her at the pinnacle; she felt the violent shudder that ran through him and then, together, they floated down into supreme contentment.

Minutes later Ashley cuddled close to Jim, secure in the circle of his arms, resting her head in the hollow of his shoulder. Beneath her ear, she heard his heartbeat slowing, beginning to resume its normal steady beat. Basking in a glorious sense of well-being, she stirred lazily against him, loving the feel of his bare skin. When he gently brushed wayward strands of hair back from her face, she tilted her head back to look up at him.

"I'm so glad you stopped fighting the inevitable," he said, moving a hand around her waist. "Any regrets, Ashley?"

"No," she answered. And it was true; she didn't have any. She loved him. Stepping her fingertips over his chest, she gave him a cheeky grin. "I just wonder if you'll still respect me in the morning."

"What do you think?"

"I think you'd better if you know what's good for you."

Laughing, he hugged her closer. "You're a delight."

"You're not so bad yourself."

"In fact, you're such a delight that . . . Come here, woman," he playfully growled, pulling her atop him, smiling at her sharp gasp. "You shouldn't be surprised. I told you I might keep you awake all night."

"Sex maniac," she called him, but her smile faded when his muscular legs slipped between hers, parting them, and he wound her hair around his hand to urge her mouth to his. Their lips met, reigniting fiery passion. And she completely forgot she had ever said she didn't want to get involved with him.

The next morning Ashley awakened to Jim's kisses. For an instant she thought she was having a lovely dream. Then memories of the night flooded in. The mere recollection of the hours of ecstasy they had shared sent an exquisite thrill rushing through her. Her body felt languid and lazy and her skin tingled, as if from the lasting imprint of his hands. Smiling sensuously, she opened her eyes and found Jim sitting on the edge of the bed beside her, clad only in a towel wrapped around his hips.

"Morning," she murmured, her voice sleepy. "You've already had a shower. What time is it?"

"About twenty to eight. You won't be late getting to your office."

"No, I'll have plenty of time," she agreed, sitting up, the sheet draped across her breasts. *"If* I get up now."

"Before you do, would you do me one little favor?"

"A favor? What . . ."

"Scratch my back," he requested with comical urgency. "It's itching like crazy. Gets that way sometimes during cold weather."

"Hmmm, well, turn around so I can reach you," she instructed, smiling to herself.

"You can do it a little harder than that," he told her wryly after her fingers had moved up and down along his spine a couple of times. "I'm not fragile, so don't be afraid you're going to hurt me."

"Yes, O master," she joked, scratching harder.

"Ah, that's much better. You're kinda nice to have around."

"Well thanks a—" Ashley began, her retort halted abruptly by the ringing of the telephone. Knowing such an early-morning call might mean trouble, she sighed as she reached over to the bedside table to pick up the receiver. After answering, she listened for a second, then handed the phone to Jim. "For you. Your service."

He nodded. "I called in from the airport last night

and left your number." After speaking to the caller, he said nothing for several moments except, "Yes. I see." Then, "Which hospital is he in? All right. I'm on my way." He hung up quickly, stood and looked down at Ashley. "One of my new patients—overdose of sleeping pills he managed to find somewhere. Manic-depressive. I've been having tests done on him for a workup, hoping I could begin lithium treatment, but . . . Damn, if the results had gotten back to me already, maybe this crisis could have been avoided."

"How is he?" Ashley asked while Jim hurriedly started to dress. "How many pills did he take?"

"No idea. His mother found him in time and called an ambulance. The message from the resident on duty is that he seems to be slowly regaining consciousness."

"Thank God for that."

"Yes. Ashley, I have to go," Jim declared, pulling on his socks, then stepping into his shoes. He walked back to the bed, buttoning his trousers. "I want to be there when he wakes up."

"Of course, I understand. You should get there as soon as you can. Your shirt and jacket are in the living room. Remember?"

"I remember," he murmured, bending to give her a rushed kiss that just barely hit her lips. Then without another word he left the bedroom, all his thoughts clearly on his patient.

Less than a minute later Ashley heard him close the front door on his way out, and suddenly she felt ridiculously lonesome. He hadn't said anything about seeing her again, hadn't even told her he'd give her a call, and she couldn't help wishing he had done one or the other.

CHAPTER SIX

Early that afternoon Ashley treated her sister to lunch at Renaldo's, a cozy restaurant they both liked. Sitting across the small round table from Colette, she studied her face carefully, then announced, "You look more cheerful today. Any special reason?"

"Well, maybe. At least I'm taking your advice and going to my first group therapy session tonight." The older sister plowed her fingers through her dark strawberry-blond hair and sighed. "I'm not all that sure therapy's going to help, but just deciding to go makes me feel like I'm doing something positive."

"And you are. It's better than sitting home moping. And I think the therapy will be very helpful," Ashley said, mischievously wrinkling her nose. "I won't tell Dad you expressed such doubts about the effectiveness of our profession."

"Oh, well, you know I didn't mean it like that at all," Colette protested, laughing. "It's just that . . . well, I grew up with a father who's a psychologist and now my sister's one too. I should have learned enough from the two of you to have my head on straight by now. I feel funny having to go to a therapist."

"You shouldn't. Sis, psychologists go to psychologists sometimes. Psychiatrists analyze each other. We can be objective dealing with other people's problems, but it's not that easy when it comes to our own personal lives. After all, we're only human," Ashley said, staring down at her aperitif, pushing a sliver of smoked salmon around on her plate with her fork. "Too human sometimes, believe me."

"All right, what gives?" Colette questioned. "You've been unusually quiet since we got here. Something wrong?"

Ashley shook her head. "No. Nothing's wrong."

"Cigarette?" her sister offered, lighting her own.

"No, thanks. Remember? I quit."

"That's right. Lucky you. I can't give them up."

"You haven't really tried yet."

Colette made a face at her. "Ex-smokers can be so sanctimonious. Don't you be like that. I'm in no mood for a sermon, especially if you're preaching it just to avoid my question. If something's not wrong, why are you so quiet today?"

"Just a lot on my mind, I guess."

"Such as?"

"Oh, this and that." Shrugging, Ashley raised her eyes.

"Oh dear, it's a man," Colette guessed. "I'd know that look anywhere. I've seen it often enough in the mirror. But how did this happen? Aren't you the one who said you didn't want to get involved with anybody for at least a year or two?"

"That's what I said all right." Sitting back in her chair, twisting a strand of hair round and round one finger, Ashley smiled ruefully. "But what we say we want and what we get are sometimes two entirely different things. And that's what happened to me. I am involved now, and I think I could use some advice."

"Lord, I hope you're not expecting to get any from

me." Colette nearly hooted, her grin not quite masking her insecurities. "I'm a two-time loser."

"You are not a loser," Ashley replied emphatically, eyes snapping. "I don't want you to think that about yourself because it isn't true. Two mistakes don't make you a loser. And I think you can advise me because you know more about men than I do, even if you haven't found the right one yet."

"And this man of yours? Do you think he's the right one for you?"

"Oh, hell, I don't know. I just know I'm in love with him."

"Is he in love with you, too?"

"He hasn't mentioned love. But I can tell he cares about me."

"So what's the problem?"

Ashley had to laugh. "Well, for one thing, he's Dr. Jim Saxon, the psychiatrist who's so opposed to radio programs like mine. You heard Dad and me talking about him the other Sunday, didn't you?"

"Yes. Oh, God, little sister, you really know how to walk into a mess, don't you?" Colette exclaimed softly, her expression incredulous. "All men are trouble. How could you let yourself get involved with one who's an enemy from the start?"

"I try not to think of him that way. We're not enemies; we just have a difference of opinion professionally," Ashley said tersely, then her tone gentled as she added, "You sound so bitter. I wish you wouldn't see all men as enemies. You're not being fair to yourself or most of them when you do."

"Damnit, you're right. I shouldn't have said that to you," Colette said contritely, crushing her cigarette in the ashtray. She shrugged. "I'm sorry. I'm still a little down on men in general, so don't pay any attention to me. Jim Saxon must have a lot of good points if you're in love with him."

"He's a very nice, intelligent, sexy man," Ashley said with a quirk of her eyebrows. "A little opinionated sometimes, but then so am I, I guess."

"Just take your time, Ashley. Don't rush into anything the way I always have," Colette advised, then turned on a happy face as she looked across the restaurant. "Oh, good, here comes our lunch, thank heavens. I'm starved. Aren't you?"

Nodding, Ashley murmured her thanks to the waiter who served her shrimp scampi.

During the remainder of the afternoon Colette's remarks lingered in her mind, although they shouldn't have. She knew what had motivated them—disappointment and disillusionment her sister hadn't had a chance to overcome yet. To make matters worse, one of Ashley's patients failed to show for his appointment without bothering to cancel, leaving her with fifty free minutes. At first she seized the opportunity to review other patients' files, but she soon found her heart wasn't really in that task. She kept hoping Jim would call her; she hadn't heard a word from him all day. And although her telephone rang four times during the fifty-minute interval, it was never Jim.

After her last appointment she gathered her coat and purse, ready to head home, but as she started out the door the phone rang once more. She answered it, then sighed inwardly when the voice on the other end turned out not to be Jim's—again. Instead it belonged to the owner of the radio station that broadcast her program. He said he'd like to talk to her immediately. Glancing at her wristwatch, she saw it wasn't quite six yet. She had time to drop in at the station and told him she'd be right over.

Fifteen minutes later she approached the receptionist's desk. "Hi, Mary Beth. Mr. Meredith asked me to come see him."

"Oh, yes. He's in his office, expecting you. You can go on down there. End of the hall. You know where it is?"

"Yes." Ashley glanced around. "Before I go, though, do you know where Nelson is?"

"He had to step out for a minute or two. But if it's important, I can try to track him down."

"No, no, that's okay. I'll see him later." Ashley started down the corridor. Mere curiosity had made her want to see Nelson; she had intended to ask him why Mr. Meredith had called her to see her, but it really wasn't important. At the end of the hall, she knocked at the door, then heard Perry Meredith ask her in. Smiling, she entered as he stood to motion her into the chair before his desk. Silver-haired, his nose a little too crooked to be considered patrician, he had always been pleasant to Ashley. At her ease, she took a seat, smoothing her skirt over her knees while he sat back down too, a thumb and forefinger tugging at his chin.

"Well, now, I thought we'd better have a little talk," he began, pulling at the knot of his tie. "It's about your program. Now, I think it's fine but . . . er . . . as you know, there are people who don't agree with me. For example, Dr. Jim Saxon. I believe you've had some encounters with him and even had him here at the station to talk to one of your callers who turned out to be a practical joker?"

"Yes, I know Jim," she answered simply.

"And you know how he feels about programs like yours?" Perry asked unnecessarily, then put up his hands. "Well, I happened to see him on the Callahan show night before last and I understand he's going to appear on two other syndicated shows in the next couple of weeks. He seems to be creating quite a controversy about radio psychologists and that could cause us some problems, if you know what I mean."

"Not exactly. If you could be a bit more specific . . ."

"The fact that he's going public with his opposition is causing other psychiatrists and psychologists to voice their agreement with him. He's not alone in his opinion, you know."

"I'm aware of that. Dr. Saxon and some of his colleagues believe some call-in hosts give listeners the impression that every problem in the world can be solved by a simple answer, which isn't true. And I try to make my audience understand that."

"As I said, I think you do a fine job."

"But?" Ashley prompted, squaring her shoulders. "You obviously called me here to say more than that."

"Yes. As I'm sure you know, we have to have a license from the FCC to be able to operate this station. And to keep that license we have to provide programming for the public good."

Lifting her chin a fraction of an inch, she nodded. "I know there are regulations, but I don't think you really believe my program is breaking any of them, do you?"

"I don't. Certainly not," Perry Meredith hastily assured her, but he still continued to tug at his chin. "Hearing respected professionals like Dr. Saxon say that these programs might cause more harm than good does worry me, though."

"Why don't we stop beating around the bush?" Ashley suggested, her level tone masking a surge of resentment. "Are you canceling my show?"

"I'm thinking about discontinuing it," Meredith reluctantly admitted. "I don't want to cancel it. The program is very popular, and advertisers are willing to pay top dollar for commercial slots on it." Slapping his hands down on the armrests of his chair, he shook his head. "Well, I have to discuss the problem with my partner and find out what he thinks about it before reaching a final decision. I just thought you ought to know that cancellation is a possibility."

"I appreciate your telling me," was her polite answer. "But I do have a few things to say about the whole situation. Dr. Saxon and some of his colleagues are right—some psychologists doing radio shows do seem irresponsible, but I'm not one of them. Before I ever agreed to do this program I told you that I didn't hope to help people with severe emotional disturbances over the phone. I tell my listeners that frequently, and they seem to understand. Most of my callers have minor problems and I can and do help them with those. I advise the ones who are obviously more disturbed to get therapeutic treatment, and if that's not providing programming for the public good, I frankly don't know what is."

"I couldn't agree more," Meredith said, rising behind his desk, smiling as she also stood. "And that's why this is such a difficult decision, one I wish I didn't have to make. But I do have to give it careful thought because getting embroiled in any kind of controversy means you're swimming in treacherous waters."

It was a valid point, and Ashley nodded as she walked to his office door, smiling ruefully as he followed. "Well, thanks for the warning."

He patted her shoulder. "Hope you understand this is nothing against you?"

"I do. When do you think you'll make your decision?"

"Oh, it'll be a few weeks. My partner's vacationing in Tahiti, and I think the problem can wait until he gets back. I don't want to interrupt his holiday with something that isn't a real emergency."

"Then I'll be on the air tomorrow night as usual," she said, stepping into the hallway. "Good night, Mr. Meredith."

"Good night. Sorry about all this."

Her parting smile was resigned as she walked back down the corridor toward the reception area. She didn't blame Perry Meredith for the misgivings he was having. She blamed . . . No, maybe *blame* was too harsh a word. But Jim was responsible for putting her program in jeopardy, which was ironic. Opposed as he was to radio psychologists, he had frequently admitted that her show was not one that troubled him. Yet it was her show that might get the ax because of his crusade, while the real offenders might very well continue broadcasting.

Breathing a silent sigh while buttoning her coat, Ashley slung the strap of her purse over her shoulder and smiled at Mary Beth at the reception desk. "Night."

"Wait," the receptionist sang out as Ashley headed toward the stairs. "Nelson's in his office now, if you still want to see him."

"It's okay. I already have the answer to the question I wanted to ask him," Ashley explained without bothering to add that she just didn't feel up to talking to anybody at that moment. She just wanted to go straight home.

Around eight o'clock that evening she sat in her living room, trying to concentrate exclusively on her embroidery. She jabbed the scarlet-threaded needle swiftly up and down through the cream linen stretched taut on the hoop she held. At her feet, Ludlow rubbed against her, meowing repeatedly without any apparent reason, which did nothing to soothe her nerves. Thinking he wanted to go out, she had twice opened the door for him. Both times he had remained close to her chair, staring at her with his huge amber eyes, silently seeming to say he preferred to stay inside. Yet he wouldn't settle anywhere for a nap as he usually did when he honored her with his presence. She had no idea what was wrong with him. He didn't act sick, considering the way he had gobbled down his dinner. He just seemed restless, and she wondered if he was simply reacting to her own mood because she felt restless too.

"Damnit," she swore aloud when she jabbed her finger with the sharp needle. Luckily the slight wound didn't bleed, and she sucked at the fingertip for a second or two, which helped ease the pain she had inflicted on herself through sheer carelessness. Tucking the needle into the cloth, she laid the hoop in her lap, her expression pensive. Since leaving the radio station, she had been depressed. Perry Meredith's news had made her unhappy. Intellectually she understood Jim's personal reasons for his crusade. But emotionally she felt betrayed. She loved him, yet he might cause her to lose her radio program. She had no idea how to confront him with this new development when she saw him again. *If* she saw him. He hadn't called all day. It was past eight o'clock and she still hadn't heard a word from him. She felt a grinding little twist of pain in her chest. What if last night had been nothing more to him than a casual one-time fling? Conflicting emotions warred within her—love versus an undeniable feeling of resentment. Worst of all, there was no clear-cut victor in the contest, and confusion reigned, making her so edgy that the moment Ludlow stretched up to sharpen his claws on a leg of the coffee table, she leaped to her feet.

"Okay, that's it, cat. You're going out," she announced, sweeping him up, ignoring his protesting meow as she carried him to the front door. "You're too restless to stay in here, and it's only drizzling outside. A little misting rain won't hurt you."

Ludlow meowed again in disagreement but she persevered, opened the door, then gasped sharply as Jim loomed at the threshold seemingly from out of nowhere.

"My God, you scared me to death," she exclaimed, pressing her free hand against her chest, her heart beating at double time. "I didn't hear you drive up."

"I'm sorry," he said. "I didn't expect you to open the door before I had a chance to knock."

"Of course you didn't," she acknowledged, beginning to gather her wits again. Bending, she set Ludlow on his paws and gave him a gentle nudge in the hindquarters with her toe. "Off you go. Come back when you've worn off a little of that excess energy." She watched the cat gingerly pick his way across the wet porch, pausing once to shake a back leg, clearly not pleased at having to tread through drops of water. She glanced back up at Jim, motioning him inside. When he moved across the threshold, she took one backward step away from him. Those conflicting feelings still battled in her. She was glad to see him—very glad, in a way—yet she couldn't completely dismiss the conversation she had had with Meredith. He leaned down to plant a kiss on her forehead, and she accepted it without reaction because she was still too bewildered to know exactly what she felt.

Jim didn't seem aware of her ambivalence. Stripping off his tie and undoing his collar button, he took a long deep breath. "Sorry I couldn't get here earlier but I had two late appointments. Trying to catch up on the ones I missed when I was in California." His dark eyes held hers. "I wanted to call you today."

But he hadn't.

"I just didn't have a free minute," he went on, rubbing his fingertips hard against his brow. "I didn't even have time for dinner. Think you might be able to rustle up something for a starving man to eat?"

Something akin to a protective instinct, born of love, surged powerfully in her. He looked so tired, and he had to be hungry. The doubts that had plagued her since talking to Meredith at once seemed insignificant compared to the deep affection she felt for Jim. She nodded. "I only had soup and a salad for dinner, so there aren't any leftovers to warm up. But I have some cold cuts. Would a sandwich do?"

"Sounds terrific. Thanks."

"Coffee?"

"Please. Black."

"I remember," she said quietly, inviting him to have a seat as she left the room to go into the kitchen.

It was only later, after he nearly wolfed down the generously filled pumpernickel sandwich she had served, that she asked, "How's your patient? Did he regain consciousness?"

Nodding, Jim folded his napkin neatly, tucked a corner of it beneath the empty plate he placed upon the coffee table, then sat back on the sofa, frowning. "Unfortunately, he woke up in a state of acute depression, suicidal tendencies as pronounced as—maybe even more pronounced than—when he overdosed on sedatives."

"I'm sorry."

"So am I. It could have been avoided. I told you he's new patient. He's only nineteen. But he's been showing signs of mental aberration for over four years. Nobody took the signs seriously. At school he was considered a typical troublemaker. At home his parents decided he was just another wild, unpredictable teenager. When his mother finally realized he had a real, severe problem, her husband said, and I quote, 'No son of mine needs to go to a shrink. He's just trying to give us a hard time. He'll get over it when he gets a little older.' Finally his mother couldn't accept that homespun theory anymore and called me for an appointment. Benjamin came to see me the first time just over a week ago—about three and a half years too late. His parents should have taken him to somebody long ago, but they didn't. And I didn't have time to get a medical workup done on him and start lithium treatment before he managed to get hold of the sedatives he took last night. It's very frustrating."

"I know it is," she commiserated. "But you'll be able to help him now. That's what counts."

Wearily he rubbed his hand over his face. "You're right, but it's been a long, hard day and I guess I'm running a little low on optimism."

"A good night's sleep will remedy that."

A rather wicked smile played over his lips, and he reached for her. "I know an even better immediate remedy. Sleep can wait," he said suggestively, his hands moving around her waist. "Right now I'm much more interested in making love."

"But Jim . . ."

"You're not going to start fighting me again, are you? After everything we had together last night?" he coaxed, then groaned when he felt her stiffen a little. "What am I going to do with you? Give me some advice, Dr. Miller. If a man called in to your radio show wanting to know how to win over a very elusive lady, what advice would you give him? Tell me, Ashley, so I'll know how to win you over."

She eased free of his caressing hands, her expression somber. "I have something to tell you—news about my show, as a matter of fact. I think you should know what might happen. And if it does, I guess you can chalk up at least one victory."

"Victory?" A puzzled frown wrinkled his forehead. "I don't understand what you're talking about. Maybe if you gave me a few more details . . ."

"There aren't really any details, just one sure fact—one of KTSG's owners is seriously considering canceling my program because of all the controversy and unfavorable publicity such shows have started getting."

"I see," Jim murmured, raking his fingers through his hair, his narrowing eyes never leaving her face. "If your show is dropped, I certainly won't consider it a victory," he said. "I never made you a target, Ashley, or tried to start a campaign specifically to get you off the air."

"No, I suppose you didn't," she answered evenly. "But you did stir up the controversy and the end result might be just the same as if you had launched a campaign against me."

"This has never been personal; I've told you that. It isn't you I oppose. It's this type of programming in general."

"Well, you've certainly done a good job of getting that message across. Perry Meredith, the KTSG co-owner who called me to his office for a little chat today, knows exactly how you feel about the issue. He knows how much media attention you're getting and he's actually a little scared the station might lose its operating license."

Jim moved his hand in a dismissive gesture. "I'm sure it'd never come to that."

"Of course it wouldn't, because there's nothing wrong with my program. It falls into the category of broadcasting for the public good. Even though Mr.

Meredith believes that as much as I do, he may decide he'd better not take any chances. And that'll be the end of 'Let's Talk.' Are you sure that won't make you feel a little triumphant?"

"Not even a little," he said emphatically, shaking his head. "Look, I can see that you're mad at me right—"

"I'm *not* mad. I do feel frustrated and aggravated." And betrayed, she mentally added, folding her arms across her chest. "I wish this weren't happening."

"I know. The possibility that you might lose your show is painful."

"Not painful, exactly. I won't be lost without a radio program to do; it's really such a small part of my life, and my practice takes up much much more of my time. But what about my listeners? The people who call in? Whether you believe it or not, I was able to help a great many of them with their problems."

"I imagine you did help some of them."

"Then don't you think it'll be ironic if I get kicked off the air while that nitwit you heard in Los Angeles— Marv or Merv Wheeler, whatever his name is—will probably go right on broadcasting and spouting useless simplistic answers that won't begin to help his callers solve their problems? I ask you. Does that seem fair?"

"No, and I hope it won't happen that way," Jim replied tersely, his jaw hardening. "But I've told you, I'm doing what I have to do, and if I have my way, Merv Wheeler will lose his show instead of you losing yours."

"We don't always get our way, though, do we? Things have a way of snowballing right out of control sometimes."

"Ashley, I don't think KTSG will cancel your show, if for no other reason than the one you mentioned the other day—it's profitable."

"If Mr. Meredith and his partner get too worried

about losing their FCC license, they'll be willing to give up a little profit," she countered. "And do you know what will happen if 'Let's Talk' is dropped? I don't think you've thought about that, but I have. If my program goes off the air, one of the other radio stations in Boulder will decide to produce their own, and it just might be hosted by someone as irresponsible as Merv Wheeler. I don't think that's what you want."

"Of course not." Stretching an arm out over the back of the sofa, Jim touched her shoulder. "Ashley, listen to me. I—damnit!" he cursed when he was cut short by the shrill pealing of the telephone on the end table behind her. Grumbling under his breath, he watched her answer it, then turn back around to hand the receiver to him.

"Your service again," she told him.

He took the call, listening more than talking, as he had that morning.

Observing him, Ashley saw fine lines of strain begin to appear around his mouth, and suddenly she longed to throw her arms around him and give comfort or love or even mere physical release—whatever he needed. He had such demanding professional responsibilities that she almost felt guilty for letting him know she was angry more than disappointed in him. Yet she had needed to confront him with her feelings, and her needs counted too. Still . . .

"All right. You can reach me there if you need to," Jim said a moment later, leaning across Ashley to hang up the phone. Instead of moving back, he remained closer, searching her vivid blue eyes, trailing a fingertip across her left cheek down to the corner of her mouth. "I have to go again. Some patient. He's a very intelligent, enterprising young man and he nearly managed to slip out of the ward about a half hour ago. Luckily an orderly spotted him starting down the stairs. He's back in his room now, asking to see me. I want to go. I've had so little time with him; if I can get him to talk tonight, I might be able to start winning his trust. You understand?"

"Yes," she murmured, wishing his slightest touch didn't send shivers of awareness all over her. Repressing inseparable feelings of love and desire, she produced what she hoped was a convincingly nonchalant smile. "You have to go."

Lightly he kissed her lips, then got up. "We'll finish talking about this later."

"I think we are finished. What else is there to say?"

"Plenty. This just might not be the right night for it. You're tired. So am I, and I may not get away from the hospital until late. Besides, I haven't been home since I got back from California. I need to unpack and get settled back in. We can talk more about all this tomorrow night."

"Jim," she began as he strode to the front door, "I . . ."

"I may not get a chance to call you tomorrow. If I don't, I'll see you tomorrow evening," he announced, giving her no chance to respond before he stepped out onto the porch, quietly pulling the door shut after him.

He walked to his car. His hand resting on the door handle, he looked back at the lighted house, seeing a shadow of movement behind the window curtains. Ashley's silhouette was vague and indistinct. He didn't want to leave her. Too much was unresolved. Yet he had no choice. Opening the car door, he lowered himself in behind the steering wheel and started the engine. He had been a doctor long enough to accept the fact that very little of his time was truly his own.

CHAPTER SEVEN

Snow flurries began drifting down onto the windshield of Ashley's car as she left the radio station Friday evening. And the weather bureau was predicting this to be only the beginning. By morning a moderate snowfall was expected in Boulder and the surrounding vicinity. Ashley didn't mind. In fact, the promise of a clean, crisp coverlet of white blanketing the city excited her. She loved snow. It brightened the world and refreshed her. She didn't even mind her nose being nipped with cold. What she did mind was the gray, dirty slush that blemished Boulder's streets as the flakes began to melt. Snow could transform any city into a beautiful icy kingdom . . . until the thaw. Actually snow in the mountains and rural areas was her ideal; there it remained pristine, unpolluted by the exhaust of cars until it melted, soaking the ground and providing moisture for the trees, the wild rambling undergrowth and the slumbering seeds of vibrant wild flowers that would blossom forth in spring.

Wishing she could be zigzagging down a ski slope somewhere tomorrow, Ashley turned off the main thoroughfare onto her street and a few moments later pulled into her driveway. After cutting the engine, she removed the key from the ignition, then found the one on the ring that belonged to her front door. Gathering her purse and leather file folder, she got out of the Camaro and started up the sidewalk toward her porch. Nearby, another car door slammed. There was always somebody coming or going in this neighborhood and she paid no attention to the sound until out of the shadows the shape of a man loomed close to her. She cried out, heart chugging like a runaway freight train.

"Ashley, it's just me," Jim exclaimed softly, slipping an arm around her waist. She immediately relaxed.

"You seem to be making a habit of scaring the daylights out of me," she uttered after catching her breath. "Give a girl a warning next time. Okay?"

"I'm sorry. I didn't mean to startle you."

"No harm done. You only took two or three years off my life," she retorted, regaining enough equilibrium to make a feeble joke. Taking another deep breath, she continued toward the porch. "Come in. No use in us standing out here in the cold."

"No use going in, either, since I'm taking you home with me," Jim announced, wheeling her around to direct her across the yard toward his car, which was parked at the curb. "We have some unfinished business to discuss. Let's go."

Her heart thundering wildly again, Ashley hung back, dragging her heels, muttering, "I can't go."

"Why not?"

"Well, for one thing, I have to feed Ludlow."

"Fine, you can leave some food for him," Jim agreed, turning her back toward her house. "Then we'll go."

"What's this all about, Jim?"

"I told you: unfinished business."

"What's the use repeating what we said last night? We've gone over the subject so many times. We're never going to be able to agree."

"Never say never," he intoned, taking the house key

from her to unlock the front door. When she preceded him inside, he playfully swatted her fanny, grinning as she jerked her head around to give him a surprised and questioning look while she switched on the living-room light. He motioned her along. "Come on. Don't dawdle. Fill Ludlow's bowl, put it where he can get to it and let's go."

Shaking her head, Ashley put down her purse and began unbuttoning her coat. "I can't, Jim. Haven't you heard the weather report? We're supposed to get several inches of snow tonight, and I can't be stranded out at your house."

"I can't get stranded at home either," he said, stepping forward to rebutton as fast as she unbuttoned. "I have appointments to keep in the morning. Remember? I told you I was trying to catch up. And I have the Jeep, so what's a little snow? I'll be able to get you back here without any problems."

"But still, I—"

"Come willingly, wench, or prepare to be abducted," he warned, imitating Errol Flynn at his devil-may-care best, right down to the tempting glint in his eyes. "Even if you fight and scratch and scream, I'm going to take you away with me."

She laughed at his talented performance. "What in the world's gotten into you?"

"You have, my darling," he professed theatrically, switching to a fairly good impersonation of Cary Grant. "Ashley, Ashley, Ashley."

"That's supposed to be 'Judy, Judy, Judy,' and I've read he never really said it in any movie anyhow," she told him, her lips twitching. "And I think you're dangerous in this mood."

"Right you are," he admitted, swiftly sweeping her

up in his arms. "Dangerous enough to resort to kidnapping if I have to."

Practically giggling, she wriggled. "Put me down, Jim. You're—"

"Say you'll come home with me and I'll let you go," he said, reverting to his own deep voice, his tone persuasive. "Just say yes, Ashley."

His lips brush-stroked hers and their warmth was more than she could withstand. She loved him. He made her happy, made her laugh, made her yearn to be with him. Unable to resist him, she whispered "Yes" at last.

His kiss lingered for several breathtaking moments before he lowered her feet to the floor and released her with a slow smile. "You aren't going to try to change your mind now, are you?"

"No. Just give me time to pour some food into Ludlow's dish and set it out at the top of the basement stairs. He has his own little swinging door, so he can get in down there whenever he wants to. You wait here. I'll be right back."

Several minutes later Ashley and Jim were on the interstate highway, leaving Boulder behind. The twinkling lights in the suburbs festooned the cloudy night, but they too soon faded away and thickets of trees rose up along the roadside. Glistening snowflakes fell faster before the headlights and upon the windshield as the flurries became a steady shower of purest white.

Cozy in the car, half hypnotized by the swirling snow, Ashley drew a contented breath and turned sideways in her seat to look at Jim. His clean-cut profile was silhouetted in the dim light of the dash. As she gazed at him, he turned his head briefly to glance at her. And when he reached over to take her hand in his, then press it down lightly upon his thigh, she felt curiously content. He had a way of making her feel like that, despite the differences between them.

When Ashley and Jim arrived at his house a few minutes later, they dashed toward the door in the blowing snow. Particles of sleet peppered their faces, and her cheeks were enchantingly rosy when they hurried in to the dimly lighted foyer. For a long moment he simply looked at her glowing features framed by shining flaxen hair. Then, reaching out, he brushed scattered snowflakes from the top of her head and her shoulders, the heels of his hands lingering a second on the inviting rise of her breasts. A flicker of light appeared in his eyes. He started to move closer but shook his head and smiled wryly instead.

"God, you can be so distracting," he declared, resolutely behaving himself as he helped her off with her coat and hung it up, though he kept his on. Guiding her into the great room, he switched on a lamp. "Make yourself comfortable. I'll start a fire before moving the car into the garage."

"How about letting me handle the fire while you go ahead and put the car away?" she suggested. "I've always liked starting fires."

His eyebrows shot up. "You surprise me. I never suspected you of harboring latent pyromanic tendencies."

"Cut the analysis, Doctor." She grinned. "I'm not a potential patient or a potential arsonist. You psychiatrists tend to jump on every little word and look for hidden meaning. Liking to sit before a roaring blaze doesn't make me a fire bug. And you should try to stop thinking so much like an analyst once you leave your office."

"I'll try to do better from now on," he vowed with mock humility on his way out of the room.

When he returned less than five minutes later, Ashley

was kneeling on the smooth stone hearth, arranging logs on the grate with a poker, moving them so that the flames licking up from the ignited kindling curled around and among them more effectively. Intent on what she was doing, she apparently hadn't heard him come back in, and he stopped in the center of the room to observe her in complete silence. The golden glow of the fire illuminated her face and burnished her hair. He saw the faint smile that adorned her lovely, soft lips, and he watched the graceful movements of her hands. Her sweater covered but didn't conceal the straightness of her spine and the arch at the small of her back that curved flowingly into the gentle swell of her jean-clad hips. She was beautiful; not a typical beauty-pageant marvel of physical perfection . . . perfect she wasn't. Her nose was almost snub and was scattered over with freckles, as were her cheeks. Her mouth was just a bit too wide. But to him she was beautiful, because an inner loveliness shone out and bathed her in warm radiance. She had an inborn quality that drew people to her. At least she drew him. He found her fascinating, and the need to be close to her was more intense than he had ever experienced with any other woman in his life. For a split second he considered going over to sweep her up in his arms and up to his bed, but he wanted more than the mere gratification of physical needs. She had much more to offer than that, and he needed all she could give, and needed to give back the same to her.

Coughing softly, he attracted her attention at last, then walked to the portable bar on his left. "How about a drink?"

"It's the perfect night for one," she answered, giving the logs one last gentle poke before rising to her feet and nodding. "I think I will have something. Do you know how to make a hot ginger fizz?"

Jim's face fell. His forehead wrinkled.

"Only kidding," she assured him, suppressing a laugh at his near-comical expression. "I just made that up; there's no such drink that I know of. But I will have a vodka and tonic, easy on the vodka, please."

"Coming up," he said, smiling lazily at her little joke as he brought forward a bottle of gin along with the vodka and tonic water. "And I think I'll join you, since I won't have to be driving again tonight."

It was Ashley's turn to raise her eyebrows. "Oh? And if you aren't planning to drive again tonight, how am I supposed to get home?"

"You aren't supposed to; that's why I kidnapped you."

"You didn't kidnap me. I agreed to come."

"See how very devious I am?" he countered, his tone villainous as he mixed their drinks. "I coaxed you into agreeing to come with me, but now that you're here, you're at my mercy."

He was kidding. She knew it. Yet a keen shiver of excitement scampered through her, skittering evocatively over every inch of her skin. Her heartbeat picked up a little and, her blue eyes wary, she watched him approach her carrying two ice-filled tumblers. With a murmur of thanks, she accepted the one he handed her as he sat down close to her on the sofa. He was so near, in fact, that she felt his muscular thigh brush against her as he settled himself comfortably, his long legs outstretched before him. She took a small sip of her drink.

He turned toward her, observing her enigmatically for several quiet moments before also taking a swallow. When he lowered the cut-glass tumbler to rest it lightly upon the arm of the couch, his expression altered and grew solemn as he murmured, "I'm sorry, Ashley."

"Sorry? About what?"

"Your radio program—the possibility that it might be canceled. That's the unfinished business we have to talk about. I want you to know that I didn't get involved in this controversy because I wanted you to be taken off the air. I got involved because of irresponsible oafs like Merv Wheeler and the damage he may be doing. I want you to believe that."

"I guess I do."

"But you're not quite sure?"

She put a hand up. "All I know is that the controversy might mean the end of my program."

"I know that too. That's why I'm sorry, although I'm only doing what I feel I have to," Jim said, concern evident in his voice. "People love to find simple answers to their emotional problems, and too many radio psychologists give pat answers that sound great but do little good. How many listeners identify with callers' problems and decide following the advice given will miraculously solve all their troubles? And how do the psychologists get a complete perspective on their callers after speaking to them for only a minute or two on the phone? They can't, and that's my point. Without studying the individual, any advice given, no matter how general, might cause more harm than good. It's comparable to telling someone with cardiovascular disease to jump into a regimen of strenuous exercise."

"No, it's not quite the same," Ashley disagreed, having listened respectfully to his opinion. "It's much easier to evaluate a person's physical condition. There are definitive tests that give precise results. Evaluating emotional health is much trickier, because even when we deal with patients on a person-to-person basis over a period of time, they can still lie to us, hide truths and feelings and give misleading information."

"True, but when we see patients face-to-face, we can

watch their facial expression, their body language, the look in their eyes. All those things help us judge them better. Then we have to probe more deeply. But when the patient is merely a voice on the phone, that's it."

"I told you before that I only deal with simple problems and I give very sound advice."

"I agree, but if that's the kind of problem you regularly deal with on your show, don't you feel more like an advice columnist on the air than a psychologist?"

"Maybe, but what's wrong with being both as long as what I do is useful?" she countered, cradling her glass in her hands. "Not everyone needs therapy, but a lot of people just need someone to talk to, someone objective. I'm not ashamed of filling that need. In fact, I'm proud I can help even a few people."

"Too bad some of your broadcasting colleagues have no reason to feel proud," Jim said, his words hard-edged. "They don't have your professional ethics, apparently, and they help no one with their smooth answers to problems that would realistically take many therapy sessions to resolve."

"I don't want to be lumped in with the likes of them; I've told you that. I'm as sorry as you are that they've been given air time to play God. But I can't control their behavior and make them have high ethical standards, and I still think it's ironic that 'Let's Talk' may be canceled, while the shows you have good reason to complain about will go right on running."

A muscle ticked with fascinating regularity in his jaw as he looked into her eyes. "Sometimes the innocent have to suffer when things are made better all the way around," he softly said. "If I could change that, even just for you, Ashley, I would, but I can't."

"I know that, but what happens when my program is dropped and one of the other stations produces a call-in show hosted by someone irresponsible? What will you do then?"

"Protest the programming every chance I get," Jim answered succinctly, his dark eyes narrowing, fervor lighting their depths. "I've never attacked 'Let's Talk' directly, but if it's canceled and another station puts on a call-in hosted by anybody vaguely resembling Wheeler, I'll be the first to launch an attack to get it off the air. Believe me."

She did. Yet nothing changed the fact that his crusade threatened a segment of her life she considered important. And she was no masochist; she loathed the idea of being an innocent victim because some dishonorable colleagues were exploiting the public. Was that her fault? No! And she refused to accept any responsibility for their lack of ethics. But that refusal didn't do anything to help resolve the differences between Jim and her. He had set his course and so had she, and they were heading in opposite directions because they were both strong willed. What could alter that? Nothing, that she could see.

Stroking her brow with stiffened fingers, she shook her head. "Let's talk about something else, why don't we? We just go round and round and round about this and never get anywhere."

Jim didn't answer immediately. He took another sip of his drink and allowed the silence to stretch out between them before he smiled. "So you want to change the subject? That's an obvious defense mechanism, Ashley."

"I thought I asked you to cut the analysis," she retorted, his lighter tone easing much of her tension. "If I ever feel the need to see a psychiatrist, I'll make an appointment with one. Right now I'm just not in the mood to rehash all this. We're sitting in front of a cozy fire, and I'd rather talk about something more agreeable."

"What do you have in mind?"

Taking another sip of her clear, sparkling drink, she raised her shoulders in a slight shrug. "Oh, I don't know. Anything, I guess. Why don't you tell me what it's like living on a cattle ranch during the winter?"

One corner of his mouth tipped upward as he eyed her suspiciously. "Is this just your way of changing the subject, or do you really want to know?"

"I want to know. I wouldn't have asked if I didn't. I've always lived in the suburbs, so I have no idea what it's like on a ranch in winter."

"Cold. The wind whips across the range and rattles the windows. It's almost stark when snow covers the ground, but beautiful too," Jim said quietly. "The nights are silent except for the wind. On the days the cattle can't graze because the ground is covered, we'd load hay onto the truck to take out to them. I started a lot of icy mornings doing just that, but it had its compensations, now that I look back. The air was always fresh and sweet and the crust of the snow had a clean squeak when we crunched over it in our boots."

"You almost sound like you miss winters like that."

"Sometimes I do, a little. When I do, I go home for a weekend and help with the chores, then come home refreshed and better able to relate to my patients without letting myself get bogged down in their problems."

She gave an understanding nod. "How big is the ranch? Is it one of those huge spreads that stretches out forever?"

"Sometimes it seems that way when we ride out looking for strays but no, it's not a huge spread compared to some. About average-size, I'd say." He smiled wryly. "In other words, we don't have a helicopter to fly out and check on the herds, like a few ranchers have. The place isn't an empire, just a typical ranch, family operated."

"It sounds very romantic, though."

"That's because you're a city girl," he teased, tapping the end of her nose. "And you've probably seen too many Westerns. There's a certain romance to it but there's also a lot of hard work."

"I guess I do tend to look at it through rose-colored glasses, probably because when I was seven or eight I was absolutely sure I wanted to grow up to be a cowgirl."

"A typical childhood fantasy. I was typical too; for a while I wanted to be a big-city police detective. But Mark, my brother, wasn't typical at all. He wanted to be a truck."

"A *truck!* You're kidding?" Ashley exclaimed softly. "You mean a *truck* truck?"

"The very same. Four wheels, a bed and a cab. That's what he wanted to be."

"I've heard about some strange childhood fantasies but that beats them all." Then she added jokingly, "Have you had Mark come in for analysis?"

"No, he's perfectly all right now. He grew out of that odd notion by the time he was seven."

"I'm glad to hear it."

"So were my parents, believe me," Jim bantered, humor flashing in his eyes. "And now that I've laid bare one of my family's darkest secrets, how about you? What about your sister? Did she want to be something as strange as a truck?"

"Not at all. I can remember a time when she wanted to grow up to become Miss America. And if she hadn't changed her mind and decided to be a voice teacher, she might have been able to make that dream come true. She's beautiful."

"Beauty seems to run in your family."

Ashley smiled. "Thank you, kind sir. You know just what to say to a woman."

"I mean it."

"But you've never seen Colette. Oh, we look a little bit alike, but she has a much nicer nose than I do."

"I happen to like your nose very much," he said. He glanced down at the glass she held. "Freshen your drink?"

"No thanks. I'm fine."

"I could use more ice," he said.

She watched him cross the room to the bar. During the past several minutes they had been getting to know each other better, and for her it was a warm, exhilarating experience. She wanted to know about his childhood and his family. Loving him, she needed to know everything. Getting up, she walked over to look out the french doors at the night, watching snowflakes hit the panes of glass. She was aware of Jim moving close behind her, then leaning around to switch on an outside light. Driven snow undulated in ripples across the terrace, carpeted the nearby woods and iced the boughs of the evergreens in white. It was a lovely scene, and Ashley was too intrigued by it for a long time to notice that the storm had gotten heavier. At last she did.

"It's really coming down out there. The weather report didn't say anything about this turning into a blizzard, but I'm beginning to wonder. Just to be on the safe side, maybe I should be getting home soon."

"Home, Ashley?" Jim questioned softly behind her. "I told you I didn't plan to take you home tonight."

Turning, she grinned up at him. "But you were just kidding. I know that."

"Do you? What if you're wrong? What if I tell you I really did abduct you?"

Her heart seemed to stop, then start again with a thundering beat. Yet even as her breath caught deep in her throat, she managed to shake her head. "I don't believe that."

"I think you should," he murmured, taking her glass away from her to place it with his on the small table next to the doors. His hands then swept over her shoulders and slowly down her arms to take hold of hers, his penetrating gaze on her blue eyes. "I want to keep you here with me all night long, Ashley."

"But you won't if I'm not willing to stay," she uttered weakly, trembling as his thumbs rubbed the backs of her hands. "If I insist on going home, you'll take me."

"Will I?" Sweeping her up in his arms, he carried her to the sofa and sat down, cradling her in his lap. "Are you sure of that?"

"Y-yes. I know you well enough to know you wouldn't want to take what isn't freely given."

"You're right. But you want to give . . . and to take, don't you, Ashley? After what we had together Wednesday night, I know I want to. And you feel the same way, don't you?" he whispered, but gave her no chance to answer as his mouth descended on hers.

CHAPTER EIGHT

"Jim." She gasped, fighting for sanity amid the tempest of electrifying sensations created by his lingering kiss. She put her hands against his hard, broad chest, but her wrists felt suddenly weak and her tensed fingers relaxed and began to move against him. His arms, hard and strong around her, gathered her closer, and her breasts yielded to the firmer line of his body. She moaned, out of breath.

"You have to stay," Jim urged, his long fingers spreading through her hair. "I want you to and you want to, don't you, honey?"

"I shouldn't. You have patients to see tomorrow . . ."

"That's all right, as long as you promise not to exhaust me completely," he teased. "You will let me get some sleep, won't you?"

She had to chuckle. "You're impossible."

"And you're irresistible," he responded, suddenly quite serious again, catching the luscious curve of her lower lip between his teeth when she kissed him. The faint fragrance of the perfume she wore was like ambrosia, making him want to devour her. Tilting her head back, he spread kisses all over her face, around her ears and down the slender stalk of her neck. With the tip of his tongue he probed the fluttering pulse beat in her throat and felt her quiver, but she was neither as hesitant nor as shy as she had been at first Wednesday night. Slender, daring fingers unbuttoned his shirt, then danced provocatively over his chest, sending shivers of delight over his skin. Desire stirred hotly in him. Wrapping his arms tighter and tighter around her, aching to feel her body's lush curves against him, he claimed her honeyed mouth, groaning deeply as she opened it eagerly to the fierce yet tender pressure of his. He tasted the sweetness deep within, his heart pounding strongly against her cushioned breasts as her tongue erotically parried the thrust of his, then tarried with feather-stroking caresses over his lips.

"Sweet, you're so sweet," he murmured roughly, his questing hands roaming over her as her thighs pressed against his side. "And so warm."

She felt exceedingly warm, even feverish as his palms cupped the rounded curve of her buttocks and his lightly kneading fingers heated her flesh through the denim. He held her closer, and she lowered her head, her hair falling forward over her cheeks like a silken curtain as she pushed his shirt open wider to bestow skittering kisses on his smooth, bronzed shoulders and the skin over his collarbone. Aroused by the low-rumbling sound of pleasure he made, encouraged to continue, she grazed her hands outward over his midriff and around his lean sides to clasp them together across the small of his back, rotating her thumbs in slow, evocative circles against him. Muscle flexed beneath her touch, bringing a smile to her lips. Reveling in the power of her femininity, she toyed with his flat, hard-tipped nipples, lazily circling them with her tongue.

"Temptress," he said, tilting her head back to gaze down at her, his eyes heavy-lidded and smoldering. "Seductress."

"Not me. You started this seduction by kidnapping me."

"You don't seem to mind being abducted."

"Would you like me to put up a struggle? All right then." Amusement lit her face as she began to squirm and push against him. "Let me go, you brute! Unhand me this instant!"

"Never. You're mine now and it's impossible for you to get away." Assuming a villainous expression, he chortled victoriously. "I'm not going to let you go, my lovely, so you might as well surrender."

His arms, hardening like bands of steel, easily stilled her playful attempts to escape his embrace. Relaxing, she laughed up at him. "You're fun to be with."

"I've been trying to tell you that since we met. Glad you finally noticed," he said, gently tickling her. "I knew I could prove you're ticklish."

"No, stop," she protested, wriggling again. "That makes me crazy."

"Ummm, I can tell."

"You're—a devil!"

"Yes," he whispered, kissing her once, twice, then again slowly.

Ashley's heart jumped. The laughter died in her throat, and she wound her arms around his neck, straining nearer to him, her parted lips clinging to the firm shape of his. A current of passion ran through them, fusing them together, two hearts beating rapidly in unison, their breaths mingling. Suddenly everything was different. The moments of light banter had ended and they couldn't get close enough to each other to assuage their mutual rising need. Outside, snow fell silently; the only sound was made by the wind whispering through the boughs of the evergreens and quietly rattling the leafless branches of the aspens. Inside the great room the blazing fire sizzled and popped, but the heat emanating from the leaping orange-blue flames seemed chilly compared to the inferno consuming Ashley and Jim.

"Yes," she breathed, her entire body atingle when he pushed up the front of her sweater to caress her breasts. And, moving pliantly against him, she said nothing at all as his fingers sought the snap in the waistband of her jeans. His hand fell away and she felt a rush of disappointment, but that didn't last long because he swiftly lowered her feet to the floor, stood her up and rose next to her, his melting gaze burning over her from head to toe.

"Let's go upstairs," he said, slipping an arm around her waist to guide her out the door.

On the landing she cupped his face in loving hands when he bent to kiss her. Then they were in his lamp-lit room beside his bed. Stroking the golden cap of her hair, he grazed his lips over her temples, down her cheeks, along the delicate line of her jaw to her chin, then captured her feathering fingers in his as they drifted over his hair-roughened chest. He glanced sideways at the cold stone fireplace. "Wait, love. I'll get a fire going."

"You already have," she murmured, smiling sensuously in response to his smile as he moved away.

Logs were already arranged in the grate. It took only the striking of a match to set the kindling ablaze. Watching Jim as he bent over the hearth, Ashley removed her ankle-high suede boots and dug her stockinged toes into the thick rug beneath her feet. Acutely aroused sensual awareness made her pulses throb.

Swaying fingers of fire darted up from the kindling. Sure the logs would catch, Jim straightened and turned to look at Ashley. At his bed, she stood watching his every move, her china-blue eyes issuing an invitation he had absolutely no desire to refuse. Images of the hours they had shared Wednesday night filled his mind, and he went to her, wanting to make tonight even more a delight. Stopping in front of her, he shook his head and stilled her hands when she started to pull off her plum-color sweater.

"Let me, Ashley. I want to undress you," he murmured. He eased the sweater over her head and tossed it carelessly over his shoulder, his gaze on her as her hair settled back in glorious disarray. Unhurriedly he undid the back hooks of her pink bra, slipped the straps off her shoulders and removed it completely, giving it, too, a quick toss, his eyes never leaving her for an instant. Her upper body was an exquisite work of art, which he ached to caress and make totally his.

Standing half naked before him, feeling his hot gaze upon her, she experienced a rush of emotion so intense she trembled. Jim was the man she loved. He wanted her, and she wanted him. In that moment he could have asked anything of her and she would gladly have given. His hands moved toward her bare breasts. She watched his strong fingers move over her flesh and inscribe concentric circles to the very pinnacles of her peach-tinted nipples. Then his fingers dipped down to glide beneath her waistband and open the snap and slowly lower her zipper. He pushed her jeans down over her rounded hips, shapely thighs and long legs. She stepped out of them and also the panty hose he stripped down. The muscles of her abdomen fluttered when he started to lower the elastic band of her pink bikini briefs.

"Wait," she whispered, pulling his shirt off his shoulders, her fingers lingering on his heated flesh. "I want to take your clothes off too."

Which she did with such deliberate slowness she

nearly drove him mad. When she at last removed his last article of clothing, he threw back the covers on the bed and lowered her onto the mattress, stripping her totally naked, then drawing one hand upward between her legs and hearing her quick intake of breath as it met her feminine warmth. Resting on one elbow beside her, he swooped down to cover her lips with his while moving his hand up over her breasts, his fingers gently massaging her firm yet resilient flesh as she stroked his shoulder, arm and hip, her fingertips moving with kitten softness over his sensitized skin.

Opening her mouth a little wider to eagerly receive the imperative invasion of his tasting tongue, Ashley curled an arm around him, urging him closer and closer. Passionately giving him back kiss for kiss, she thrilled to his nearness and adored the feel of his long, hard body. She moaned in protest a moment later when he suddenly imprisoned both her wrists in one powerful hand and pressed them down above her head into the fluffy pillow upon which her hair spread in a golden fan. He was denying her the right to touch, and she ached to caress every inch of him.

"Jim, let me go," she uttered huskily against his cheek. "I want to hold you."

"And you will. I want you to. But first I have to make you want me."

"But I do."

"Not enough," he claimed, holding her fast, keeping her his prisoner. Kneeling next to her, he trailed nibbling kisses upon the tops of her feet, over her ankles and shins, then along her inner thighs, alternating from one to the other. His searching lips and teeth skipped upward to claim her full breasts, tormenting the receptive surface of her skin before drawing first one succulently erect peak, then its twin, deeply into his mouth.

Then his lips retraced their journey, pausing to linger on the taut surface of her abdomen before wandering a downward path. Parting her legs, he touched her, kissed her.

The world began spinning. Ashley closed her eyes but still it spun, heightening desire. Need licked up in her, uncontrollable flames that burned white-hot and opened a searing emptiness in her. Jim's every touch and caress, his every intimate kiss, drove her wild. She moved sinuously, lost in pleasure that was building, building . . .

Raising himself, Jim took swift, sure possession of her mouth, whispering, "You do want me now, don't you?"

"So much," she whispered back. "I want you so much."

"Show me," he commanded, releasing her wrists. "Show me how much."

Her hands floated down, encountering potent masculinity as he moved above her. She stroked, caressed and when he pushed her knees up and lowered himself between, she guided him to her, sighing softly as he entered her with a gentle thrust, feeling his shuddering tension as their bodies merged as one. Accepting his powerful, hard body, she embraced him happily, without inhibition.

For several long moments he was still. He lifted himself up on his elbows to look down at her. "Ashley, open your eyes," he murmured hoarsely. "Look at me."

She did, her bemused gaze searching the fathomless depths of his. Curving her hands over his shoulders, she raised her head off the pillow to kiss him. "Love me, Jim," she sighed. "Love me now."

"Oh, I'm going to," he vowed, beginning to move within her. "For a very long time."

Meeting each of his slow, rousing strokes eagerly, she moved loving fingers over him, feathering designs on his back, his sides and his muscularly taut bottom. Their lovemaking was sweet, unrushed, sometimes playful. She took the lobe of his left ear between her teeth, nipping lightly and smiling as he shivered with delight.

"Ashley," he murmured, his deep voice muffled in her hair. "That makes me wild."

"Yes, I remember."

"You'd better be careful. I know some tricks of my own."

Recklessly she kept on nibbling.

"Don't say I didn't warn you," he moaned, withdrawing to flip her onto her stomach. Moving astride her, he slipped his hands under her to cup her breasts and proceeded to kiss every inch of her back, then to follow the line of her straight spine with devilish little flicks of his tongue until she, too, shivered. "Yes, I know *this* makes you wild."

He was right, and it was a wonderful wildness she felt, a glorious celebration of the senses. Getting to know his body and letting him know hers gave her such emotional as well as physical satisfaction. She couldn't imagine any other man in the world evoking the feelings he did in her—a combination of love, respect and the added spice of sexual longing. Only Jim could make her feel all that, and it was only Jim she wanted. His mouth brushed over her shoulder blades, his breath tickling her skin, and she whispered, "Oh, that feels good."

"You like it?"

"Yes."

"And do you like this too?" he softly asked, pushing her hair away from her nape to kiss her there. "Hmmm?"

"Yes, yes, I like that too," she murmured, turning over between his knees to smile sensuously at him while reaching up to link her fingers around the back of his neck. "I like . . ."

"What?"

"Everything you do."

"I like everything you do too, love," he said, unclasping her hands to draw them down over his chest, where they remained to caress when he bent lower to press his lips against the soft ivory underside of her breast. "And I can never get enough of touching you. Your skin's so smooth, so firm and irresistibly delicious."

He closed his teeth gently on the erect morsel of flesh tipping one nipple, then its mate, again and again, causing her breath to come in soft little gasps as sensations flew like whistling arrows through her, plunging to her very center. Moaning, she lightly raked the edges of her nails over his ribs. She lifted her knees, parted her legs, then straightened them outside his, bringing him between. The soles of her feet drifted down over his muscular calves to his ankles, the hair on his legs tickling her.

Forsaking her breasts, Jim looked down at her. "My sexy lady," he declared possessively, a muscle working in his tightened jaw. "I always knew there was tremendous passion brewing beneath that cool professional exterior."

"You think I want you enough now?"

"Do you?"

"More than anything," she confessed, her hands on the small of his back urging him downward. "You wanted to make me want you more than I did; you succeeded. I need you, Jim."

"You can't need me as much as I need you. It's impossible," he whispered, holding her face between his hands as he lowered himself.

Ashley's lips sought his and she arched to receive the tender, deep-plunging invasion of his hard body that joined them as one again. Slowly rotating her hips, she moved in perfect synchronization with him, her inner thighs quivering, her heart thundering at a pace that matched his as ripples of pleasure became exquisite riptides. Swept up together from plateau to rising plateau of ecstasy, they exchanged dizzying kisses and muffled endearments. Intimate closeness bonded them. Loving him and knowing he cared, Ashley rode an emotional high inseparable from physical bliss, tangling her legs with his as they soared higher and higher together. Jim held her yet tighter, and she wrapped herself around him as rapture rose in quickening, pitching waves that soon crested in her with piercing sweetness. Tumbling over the culminating finely honed edge, she took him over with her, and with release they were free-falling down into consummate completion.

The warm aftermath was as fulfilling as their lovemaking had been. On their sides, holding each other, they whispered lovers' words that meant nothing yet meant everything.

Jim kissed Ashley's nose, cheeks and lips.

She cuddled close to him.

With a brushing hand, he smoothed her tangled hair.

She lightly scratched his back, garnering murmurs of deep appreciation.

Looking deeply into her eyes, he smiled lazily.

She smiled back, nestled even nearer, allowed her eyelids to flutter shut and drifted off to sleep content.

The next morning Ashley awoke before Jim. Not wanting to disturb him, she quietly raised herself on one elbow. Leaning over him, she surveyed his lean face. A day's growth of beard roughened his jaw, and the rapid eye movements beneath his closed lids told her he was dreaming. But what about? Perhaps her? Wishing, hoping with all her heart that he was, she scooted silently off the bed. Her clothes were scattered all over the room and, gathering them up, she smiled reminiscently, thinking of how urgently he had undressed her, then cast every garment away. Her gaze wandered back to the bed. She was sorely tempted to go back and wake him up. But no, if she did that she knew what would be likely to happen, and he needed his rest, since he had patients to see this morning. With a regretful smile she tiptoed into the adjoining bathroom, reached in over the glass-enclosed tub and turned on the shower, adjusting the water temperature until it was pleasantly hot, perfect for a cold morning. Glancing out the bathroom window, she saw scattered flakes of snow still drifting down and shivered. After wrapping a royal-blue towel in a turban around her head, she stepped into the tub beneath the warm spray and pulled the glass door shut.

Singing softly to herself, she smoothed a frothy layer of soap lather all over herself, inhaling its clean, fresh, perfumeless fragrance. Steam swirled around her as she washed, and finally she moved directly beneath the showerhead and turned slowly around and around, allowing the water to pepper her breasts and back as she rinsed. Still singing a decade-old love ballad, humming whenever she forgot the words, she shut off the faucets, pushed the glass door back on its steel runner and stepped out of the tub onto a plush rust-color mat. Picking up the large blue body towel she had laid out, she started patting herself dry, then held the ends in both hands to rub it up and down and back and forth over her back. She was drying her legs when there was a soft knock at the bathroom door.

"Morning," she called, removing her turban and

shaking her head. Feathery tendrils of hair clung to her damp cheeks. "Be out in a second."

"Are you dressed yet?"

"No, but—"

"Good," was Jim's quick answer as he flung open the door, stepped across the threshold and raised a camera in front of his face. "Smile, honey."

She didn't smile; she gasped as she heard a click and was momentarily blinded by a bright flash. Then her mouth literally dropped open. *"What are you doing?"* she squeaked, staring at Jim incredulously as her vision slowly returned to normal. She slowly shook her head back and forth. "You can't take a picture of me—*naked!*"

"Ah, but I just did," he retorted, the corners of his mouth twitching. "It's too late to stop me now."

"No it isn't!" she exclaimed, taking a step toward him. "Give me that camera."

"No way." Grinning, he stepped back, turned around and strode across the bedroom. "I'm going to treasure this picture of you."

"You—*devil!* You have to give me that camera now." Wrapping the towel in a haphazard sarong around herself, she made a mad dash out of the bath after him, not catching sight of him until she swung out of his room into the hall and saw him poised at the top of the stairs. Still grinning, he jogged lithely down the steps, clad in a terry bathrobe, and she raced after him.

He didn't move as fast as he could have, yet he eluded her at every turn downstairs. When she rushed into the dining room, she saw the kitchen door swinging shut. She followed him in there but he was already gone. She hurried to search the great room. Empty. And realizing he was only going fast enough to keep a few steps ahead, she ran across the entrance hall into his study. He *had* to be there, unless he had sneaked back upstairs. Sure enough, after she had stepped into the room lined with medical books and professional journals, she heard a noise behind her and spun around. He was backing out the doorway, and she marched toward him, head held high.

"You have to give me that camera," she insisted, holding out a hand. "Right now."

"I'm not going to," he replied calmly, moving the camera behind his back. "I want to keep this picture of you."

He was only teasing. She knew it. She could see the laughter dancing in his black eyes. He would hand the camera over eventually. He just wanted to make her believe otherwise for a while. Shaking her head, she tried to suppress a smile. "You wouldn't dare take that film to be developed."

"I don't have to. I process my own film. I'm an amateur photographer, remember? I have my own darkroom down in the basement."

"I don't care. You're not going to develop *that* picture of me," she said, feigning supreme confidence. "I can't let you. How do I know you won't use it to blackmail me someday?"

"Still don't trust me, do you, honey?" he murmured, sadly shaking his head. "Do you really think I might be capable of blackmail?"

"No," she admitted, hitching up the towel that had slipped down over the round curve of her breasts. "And I know you're playing a game with me. You're not really going to develop that picture."

"How can you be so sure?"

"I just am. Now, give me the camera and let me expose the film to light."

He shook his head.

"Jim, you have to. I—I can't let you keep a picture of me naked like that. I'd feel funny knowing you had it."

His eyebrows shot up. "You don't seem like a Puritan, especially in bed."

"Maybe not, but in some ways maybe I am. Now stop this nonsense and give me that thing. I know you're going to sooner or later," she stated flatly, her arm flying out to try to reach around him.

He backed away, whipped the camera around in front of him again and pushed a sliding lever forward. The camera opened, exposing an empty interior. Holding Ashley's surprised gaze, he shrugged nonchalantly. "See, no film. No picture. Nothing to worry about anyway."

He had tricked her. And she had fallen for the joke hook, line and sinker. Half amused, half irritated, her fists clenched, she glared at him. "You—you—"

"Now, now, now, no name calling."

Blue eyes narrowing, she stalked toward him.

He made no move to back away. Instead he put the camera down on the desk at the door and advanced in her direction, pulling the towel from around her when they met, smiling as she gasped, her heart pumping wildly as his hands skimmed over her breasts.

"Let's go back to bed," he whispered, lowering his head to languidly kiss her lips. "Why should I need a picture of you when I can have you in the flesh? If you're willing . . ."

"I . . . But you have appointments to keep this morning."

"It's early and the first one isn't until ten. We have all the time in the world," he promised, leading her into the foyer and up the stairs. On the landing he stopped and turned her to him, enfolded her in his arms and whispered in her ear, "After I see my patients this morning, we'll spend the rest of the weekend together. Okay?"

She nodded, never for a moment considering saying no.

Enslaved by explosive passion, needing to be one with her again, he lifted her and carried her down the hall.

CHAPTER NINE

Coming back from lunch early Tuesday afternoon, Ashley found Jim waiting for her in her office, wandering around, examining the titles of the books on her shelves. He smiled as she walked through the door.

"The receptionist, Polly, told me you were here," Ashley said, removing her coat while she walked over to him, smiling happily when he bent to give her a brief kiss. "This is a pleasant surprise. What brings you by?"

"The message you left with my receptionist this morning."

"Oh, but it was nothing urgent; you didn't have to come over. You could've just called me back."

"I had lunch with an old friend at Flagstaff House, and since I was in the area I decided to drop in to see you on my way back to the office."

After hanging up her coat, Ashley motioned Jim to one of the cornflower-blue chairs opposite the sofa where she conducted group therapy sessions. She tucked her purse away into a desk drawer, then went to sit on the sofa across from him, poised on the edge of the cushion, her elbows resting on her knees, her chin cupped in her hands. "Been waiting for me long?"

"Not very. About five minutes."

"I meant to get back earlier, but I had lunch with Colette."

"And how is she? Less depressed, I hope."

"Maybe a little, but I'm still worried about her. She's always been such a confident person, but now . . ." Ashley sighed. "She's always belittling herself these days. She's gone to group therapy twice, and all she could say was that she was the only divorcée in the group who was a two-time loser and that made her feel she didn't belong."

"She's been disillusioned twice. She feels like a failure. You're her sister and you feel her pain, but you have to remember she's like everyone else—she needs time to regain confidence in herself. With help she will, sooner or later."

"I hope it's sooner."

"So do I," Jim said sincerely, then consulted his wristwatch. "I have to get going soon; my next appointment's in twenty-five minutes. Want to tell me what you called me to talk about this morning?"

"I just wanted to tell you I've changed my mind about us having dinner out tonight."

"Why?" he questioned, a flicker of impatience passing over his face. "For God's sake, you're not going to start playing hard to get again, are you?"

"Me?" She placed a hand against her chest. "I've never played hard to get."

"The hell you haven't. I—"

"Hold it, hold it. You're jumping to conclusions," she put in, smiling wryly. "I said I'd changed my mind about us going out to eat. I've decided to make dinner for us at my house, if that's okay with you. I make fantastic barbecued ribs." She smiled. "It's my own secret recipe and I won't tell you what it is even if you beg me since you wouldn't tell me the secret ingredient in Saxon's chicken supreme."

Jim's displeasure vanished. Grinning, he stood,

reached down for her hands and pulled her to her feet, brushing his lips against hers. "One of these days maybe we'll both compromise and decide to share the recipes," he suggested before striding away from her to the door. He glanced back over his shoulder. "Barbecued ribs sound great. I'm looking forward to them. See you at your house around seven. All right?"

"Perfect," she replied. After he left her office, shutting the door after him, she wrapped her arms around her waist, hugging herself. She felt the strongest urge to do a little pirouette and at last gave in to the impulse and did it, watching her softly shirred wool skirt swirl prettily around her knees. Then she shook her head, bemused. Being in love could make anyone a little crazy with happiness.

Taking control of herself, she checked the time and found she had over fifteen minutes until her first afternoon appointment. She went to her desk, sat down and started to catch up on some paperwork. There was a knock on her door in Polly's distinctive light tapping, and when the fortyish receptionist entered the office, Ashley gave her a smile.

"There's a reporter outside asking to see you," Polly announced, wrinkling her nose with some obvious disdain. "From the Boulder *Record*."

Ashley made a little face. The *Record* was hardly her favorite newspaper. It was just too sensational, so she rarely read anything printed in it and she wasn't particularly eager to see their reporter. "What does he want, Polly? Did he say?"

"Something about interviewing you about your radio program. I thought you might want to talk to him."

"Guess I'd better," Ashley murmured with a soft sigh. "Thanks, Polly. Send him in."

Scarcely a second later a stringy man in his thirties

with closely cropped ash-blond hair presented himself in the doorway, then swaggered across the office, a broad smile on his face. "Dr. Miller?"

Smiling back politely, she nodded. "And you're . . ."

"Benton Hall the third," the reporter introduced himself. "Scooter, to my friends. I'm with the *Record*."

"Yes, that much Polly told me. Sit down, please," she said, moving a hand in the direction of the chair before her desk. "What is it you want to see me about, Mr. Hall?"

"Scooter, please," he insisted, that pasted-on smile still beaming. "We're going to be friends, I'm sure."

She wasn't. There was something about him—maybe it was because his smile never seemed to reach his cold gray eyes—that made her feel tense and in no mood to play name games with him. Sitting back in her swivel chair, she linked her fingers across her waist and looked directly at him. "I don't have a lot of time to give you. Sorry. I'm expecting a patient in about ten minutes, so if you'll just tell me exactly why you're here, we'll have more time to talk."

"Right, right," Hall answered, then inclined his head to the side and back toward the door. "Wasn't that Dr. Jim Saxon I just saw in the outer office a minute ago?"

"Yes, it was."

"Here to see you?"

"Yes."

"Why?" the reporter asked, practically smirking. "Surely he isn't a patient of yours?"

"Of course he isn't."

"Why was he here then? Did he come by to protest your show on KTSG again?"

"There's no reason for him to do that, since I know exactly how he feels about radio programs like mine."

"So his visit was strictly social?"

"You could say that."

"You're friends, then? I don't see how you could be when he attacks you and your radio show every chance he gets."

"People who have a difference of opinion aren't necessarily enemies."

"Then the two of you are friends?"

"Yes," Ashley answered stiffly, her voice ice-edged. Hall seemed to be interrogating her and she didn't appreciate it one bit, but she maintained an outward calm. "We're friends."

"How friendly are you? I've heard you two have been seen together in public," the pushy reporter announced gleefully. "Is that true?"

"You're not taking notes, Mr. Hall," she said, suddenly on the offensive, loathing his sneering attitude. "And unless you have a tape recorder hidden in one of your pockets, you're not getting what I'm saying down word for word."

"No problem at all. I have an incredibly good memory."

"Is it good enough for you to quote me accurately in the story you're going to do?"

"You don't have to worry about that."

"I'm afraid I do."

"Why? Do you have something to hide?" Hall's callous gray eyes crawled over her upper body. "Are you and Dr. Saxon lovers, Dr. Miller? You can tell me the truth off the record. I'm just curious and won't print your answer."

Ashley had taken all she could from this obnoxious man. Regally she stood, planted her palms firmly on her desk top and leaned forward, her disgusted gaze raking over Benton Hall the third. "Polly understood you to say you wanted to talk to me about my radio program, *not* my relationship with Dr. Saxon. And I agreed to an interview, not an inquisition. You're wasting my time, and I have much better ways to put it to use. You know the way out."

Shrugging carelessly, the reporter uncoiled out of the chair, walked to the door, then paused there to look back at Ashley, an unpleasant smile twisting his thin lips. "You may be sorry you weren't willing to cooperate with me. I'll have to write that you were evasive and refused outright to answer many of my questions."

"Do whatever you please," she said, producing a blithe smile that could have earned her an Academy Award for best actress. But the smile ceased and she uttered a curse after Hall exited her office. Determined not to let such a creep upset her for long, she took several deep breaths, sat back down to open the file of the patient she would be seeing in less than five minutes and valiantly managed to push all thoughts of Hall far back in her mind. Snakes like him weren't worth worrying about.

Ashley didn't think about Benton Hall III until after dinner that evening, as she and Jim had coffee in the living room.

"Delicious ribs—the best I've ever eaten," Jim complimented. "You promised something special and you delivered. Changed your mind yet about sharing the recipe?"

"Are you going to share yours for Saxon's chicken supreme?"

He lifted one shoulder in a resigned gesture. "If I did, Grandma might never forgive me. If it were up to me, I'd tell you right now."

"Likely story. And you can forget about getting my recipe for barbecued ribs," Ashley said lightly. "If you won't tell me how to make the chicken, my lips are sealed too."

"Maybe I should give Grandma a call soon and ask for special permission to give you the recipe. I can probably talk her into it," Jim mused, tapping a fingertip against his jaw, then nodding at her. "It's worth a try. We shouldn't keep secrets from each other."

"Speaking of secrets, our relationship obviously isn't one," she replied, suddenly remembering the overly aggressive reporter. "Did you happen to notice a man in the waiting room when you left my office today?"

"As a matter of fact, I did, right before I met your father."

Her eyes opened a little wider. Hall was momentarily forgotten. "You met Dad?"

"Introduced myself to him on my way out. He was coming back from lunch. I didn't get a chance to talk to him long, but he's a very pleasant man. He didn't tell you we met?"

"I guess he didn't have a chance. I had appointments booked back to back all afternoon and he left earlier than I did, so we didn't even see each other."

"Well, anyway, I did see the man in your waiting room. So what did Benton Hall the third—Scooter to his friends, if he has any—have to say to you?"

"You know him?"

"He came to see me yesterday for an interview," Jim explained but wrinkled his forehead questioningly. "Obviously he didn't just ask you about our difference of opinion; he got more personal. But why do you say our relationship isn't a secret, as if that upsets you? I didn't know it was supposed to be a secret."

"It isn't. I didn't mean it like that. It's just that Hall is such a despicable man, and I hated having him question me about us. He actually came right out and asked if we're lovers. Said he was only curious and wouldn't print my answer." Pressing her lips tightly together, she shook her head. "Of course he didn't get an answer at all and I told him to leave, but I wonder what kind of slanted story he's going to write."

"Don't worry about him. I'm not going to," Jim murmured reassuringly, draping an arm across her shoulders. "He isn't a talented reporter or he wouldn't be working on a newspaper like the *Record*. It has a bad reputation, to say the least, and I doubt anyone believes anything that's printed in it. Besides, the few people who read it wouldn't be very interested in our relationship. Neither of us is married, so where's the scandal? For a scandal sheet like the *Record,* we can't be very newsworthy, so try not to be upset by anything Hall said or any of the questions he asked."

"I'm not upset," she told him honestly. "But it's very easy to be mad at an absolute jackass like Hall."

"He's not worth the energy it takes to be angry," Jim said, tipping her face up. "Forget about him, Ashley."

And as he kissed her, she did.

About eight forty-five the following morning, Ashley's father came to see her in her office, knocking once on the door, then stepping in.

"Oh, morning, Dad." She greeted him brightly, pouring water into the pot that contained a lush philodendron that graced one of the shelves. Finished, she walked over to give Tom Miller a kiss on the cheek. She had to stretch up on tiptoe. He was tall; Colette had inherited her elegant height from him, while Ashley took after their mother and was of average height. But Ashley had her father's deep blue eyes. This morning his looked a bit troubled. He squeezed her shoulder almost absentmindedly, but she didn't question his mood.

She knew him well enough to realize if he had something to say, he would when he was ready.

Crossing the office, Tom settled down on the sofa and leaned forward, propping his elbows on his knees as he smiled faintly at his daughter. "I met Dr. Saxon yesterday," he said at last. "He was going out as I was coming in and he introduced himself."

"Yes, I know. Jim told me last night."

Tom nodded. "I see. Well, since you saw him last night, I guess you had better see this now," he said quietly, bringing forth the folded newspaper he had brought in tucked under his arm. He handed it to her. "First page, second section."

Opening the paper and seeing it was a copy of that morning's *Record,* Ashley felt a sinking sensation in her stomach. She sat down and immediately found the second section, gritting her teeth when she found separate grainy photographs of Jim and herself, obviously taken without their knowledge—pictures that weren't at all flattering and made them look almost like criminals. She raised her eyes, met her father's, then glanced back down to read the half-page article, angry color deepening in her cheeks with every outrageous paragraph she read.

Certain words and phrases leaped out at her, intensifying the resentment she felt. Everything Benton Hall had written was exaggerated to the point of being pure nonsense. After briefly and overdramatically relating Jim and Ashley's difference of opinion about radio psychologists, he attacked them with innuendoes.

"Dr. James Saxon, cool and calculating, attempted to explain his conflict with Dr. Miller with brusque responses . . ."

"Dr. Ashley Miller, a young attractive blonde, refused to offer any explanation whatsoever . . ."

"Saxon and Miller are frequently seen together in public . . ."

"When asked about her personal relationship with Dr. Saxon, Dr. Miller became defensive .. . ."

"Is this a true controversy? Does Dr. Saxon really object to Dr. Miller's call-in show? Or is this merely a plot, a ploy to gain publicity for Ashley Miller's 'Let's Talk,' aired three nights a week on KTSG radio. Nothing better than a seemingly heated conflict to attract more listeners . . ."

Ashley couldn't believe even Benton Hall could have manufactured such a distorted story, stuffed full of insinuations. After reaching the last word she rolled the newspaper section tightly and smacked it against her thigh, looking up at her father again, defiance glittering in her eyes. "Where did you get this piece of rubbish? I know you don't read this thing."

"No. One of Polly's neighbors gave it to her because she knows she works for us. The article upset Polly so much she showed it to me so I could decide whether or not to let you see it."

"That dirty s.o.b.!" Ashley softly exclaimed. "How could he write such trash, and how could any newspaper, even one as sorry as the *Record,* print it? It's incredible how he's twisted every little thing around to make it sound—sordid, dishonest . . . *cheap.*"

"He certainly did that," Tom Miller agreed, regarding her speculatively. "So you saw Jim Saxon last night?"

"Yes. What of it?"

"Nothing, sweetheart," he murmured, reaching over to pat her right hand, which was clenched into a fist upon her knee. "Try to relax; I wasn't criticizing."

"I know that," she said, heaving a sigh. "Sorry I snapped at you, Dad."

"After reading that you had a right to snap at somebody. But I want you to know that I liked Jim when I met him yesterday."

"Really? That's great. He liked you too."

"You sound like it's important to you for the two of us to like each other."

"I guess it is."

"Then he obviously means a lot to you?"

Ashley nodded. "He does. I . . . We're very close."

"I see." Her father smiled understandingly. "Well, your mother and I thought you must be getting involved with someone since we haven't been seeing much of you lately."

She smiled back, relaxing a little. "I didn't mean to be neglecting you."

"We don't feel neglected as long as you're happy."

"I'm almost always happy when I'm with Jim."

"A sure sign you're in love," Tom said teasingly, patting her hand once again, then inclining his head toward the rolled newspaper she still held. "But what are you going to do about that?"

"I wish I knew." She gnawed at her lower lip. "It complicates everything. It makes Jim and me seem like —frauds. What do you think I should do about it?"

"Nothing until you've thought it over carefully," her father advised, standing. "Do what you tell your patients to do: don't panic, don't feel like it's the end of the world because it isn't; just try to remain calm and work it out step by step."

"Big help you are. That's what I get for having a father who's a psychologist," she said, rising to give him a quick hug. "But you're right. I don't want to overreact. Thanks, Daddy."

"I'll send you a bill for the counseling," he retorted, blowing her a kiss on his way out of the office.

Left alone, Ashley went to place the offensive newspaper beneath her purse in the drawer of her desk. Much as she hated the prospect, she would have to show it to Jim. The article it contained maligned his professional ethics as much as it did her own.

Ashley and Jim had planned to meet at the Fleur de Lis for dinner, but early in the afternoon she called his office and left a message to have him come to her house instead, feeling privacy was what they would need when she showed him the story in the morning *Record,* if he hadn't already seen it or heard about it. She doubted he had.

She was right. He hadn't. After arriving at Ashley's house around seven that evening and accepting the brandy she offered, he took the folded newspaper she handed him. Opening it, glancing up at her when he saw their pictures spread across the front page of the local section, he sat back, jaw clenched as he began to read.

"That bastard," he muttered a few minutes later, dropping the paper to the floor with another muffled curse. "I thought Hall's story would be buried in the back pages somewhere if he even managed to get his editor to print it."

"Must have been a slow news day. Looks like we're the hottest story in the area, anyway," Ashley said, her voice strained. "Aren't you thrilled to be such a celebrity?"

"Absolutely ecstatic."

A shadow settled over her features. "Jim, what are we going to do about this?"

"Forget it."

"Oh, that's easy to say, but will the people who read it forget? I mean, Hall makes us seem like charlatans, like we're trying to make names for ourselves so we can get more patients or become media personalities. His nasty insinuations will make anybody who ever sees us together think we're a couple of fakes conspiring either to get rich or famous or both."

"And?" he prompted rather sharply. "Are you about to suggest we stop seeing each other so people won't get the wrong idea?"

"No. I—oh, I don't know what we should do." She put her hands up. "I just don't know how to handle this. What if Hall writes more stories about us and really tries hard to manufacture a full-fledged scandal?"

"Maybe he won't go that far."

"He might, though. And his editors would probably encourage him to. The *Record* has never scored high marks in the truth-in-journalism department. And you know how scandals are, Jim. Even if they're based on a pack of lies, they tend to grow all out of proportion. People get hurt."

"We aren't going to let ourselves be victimized, Ashley," Jim declared firmly. "If Hall goes on with this, we'll let our lawyers handle him and the *Record*. No newspaper wants to be hit with a libel suit. We'll be able to protect ourselves. But maybe we won't even have to. We'll just have to wait and see what happens. All right?"

Head bent, she nodded. "Guess we don't have any other choice."

"None whatsoever," he murmured, lifting her chin with one finger. His gaze softened as his thumbs drifted over the faint violet crescents beneath her eyes. "You know, I don't think any of this would be bothering you so much if you weren't tired. Your father told me you haven't taken any time off in nearly a year—not even a day or two. We're going to remedy that by taking Friday off and spending this weekend together in Vail.

Friends of mine have a place there and let me use it whenever I want to. And we'll have it all to ourselves; they're on a business trip to Cleveland until next week. How does that sound?"

"Wonderful. But we'll have to wait and go up Saturday."

"Absolutely not. We both need a *long* weekend."

"But my Friday patients—"

"Reschedule their appointments for next week. I'll do the same with mine."

She was slowly yielding to temptation, but suddenly her face fell and she struck her forehead with her fingertips. "Oh, damn, I can't go until Saturday. I have to do Friday's radio program."

"I think you can afford to miss one broadcast. Maybe your father would be willing to fill in for you. If he can't, Nelson can program something else to fill your time slot, and I'm sure he'd understand that you need a little rest and recreation, Ashley," Jim said coaxingly. "You don't want to burn yourself out, and that's easy to do in the field we're in. We deal with people's problems constantly. Some of our patients try to blame us for everything that's wrong in their lives. We're convenient scapegoats. Daily doses of all these things wear us down. You can't disagree with that."

"No, I don't. It's true. But I'm not anywhere near the point of burn-out."

"Maybe not yet, but you'll be well on your way if you go another year without taking any time off."

"Oh, but I plan to take a vacation sometime real soon."

"Start by taking a little one this weekend," he commanded softly, an inviting smile on his lips. "The house is in the outskirts of Vail and surrounded by pines. It's very rustic; you'll love it. And I heard the ski report this morning. The powder on all the slopes is deep. Imagine cruising down quiet runs, then going back to a cozy fire and hot buttered rum."

Imagining just that, she drew in a slow, deep breath and it almost seemed she could smell the clean mountain air. Jim had seduced her with words. It was impossible for her to say no. "All right, I'll go," she said at last.

"We'll drive up Friday morning. Right?"

"Right. A long weekend will be nice."

"I knew I could convince you," he said, his boyish grin producing appealing dimples in his cheeks. "I'm a very persuasive fellow."

"And modest too," she retorted, laughing as he retaliated for that remark by hauling her against him. Her arms went around him; her lips caressed his. She loved this lovable man so much.

CHAPTER TEN

Ashley and Jim arrived in Vail around noon Friday. Sunlit, Vail mountain rose majestically against the backdrop of clear blue sky. From the road Jim pointed out the pine-encircled A-frame house they'd be staying in as he drove on into town. What had once been a quaint village had grown into a petite mountain city, but the quaintness and charm had been retained. Quiet, elegantly serene and as picturesque as a hamlet in the Swiss Alps, it promised tranquillity, a refuge from the frequently hurried and harried outside world.

"We'll have lunch in town. I know a nice little inn," Jim announced, watching for pedestrians. "Then we can buy some groceries and go back to the house. Okay with you?"

"Perfect. I'm starved. I guess it's the air up here that always makes me hungry," she said, looking out her window and observing the bright red, blue, yellow or green ski togs worn by window-shoppers idly strolling along the sidewalks. She breathed an exaggerated sigh of relief. "Thank goodness fashion hasn't changed much since I went skiing last year. At least my ski suits won't look like ancient relics."

Glancing sideways at her, Jim raised his eyebrows. "Would it really matter to you if they did?"

"Not very much. They're warm and comfortable, and

besides, I can't afford to keep up with all the new styles. The world will just have to march on without me."

Smiling, Jim entered a small parking lot, found a space and killed the engine of the Jeep. He turned toward Ashley. "We'll have to walk from here to the Chalet. Mind?"

"Are you kidding? I'd walk forever for a glimpse of their menu."

"It shouldn't take us quite that long," he remarked wryly, getting out of the Jeep. Coming around, he found she had already opened her door. He took her hand as she stepped out and grinned at her. "That hungry, eh?"

"Just the mention of the Chalet started my stomach growling."

"I'm feeling a little hollow too. Long time since breakfast."

Nodding, Ashley slipped her slender fingers between his as they turned to the right down the street. Despite the silvery white rays of the winter sun, the air was frigid, and little gusts of wind threatened to cut through her quilted jacket. It was a relief to step into the Chalet and be cocooned in welcoming warmth. Better yet, they were lunching too early for the fashionable set, and since the restaurant wasn't crowded, they were immediately escorted to an out-of-the-way table. A waiter soon appeared, and they each had a glass of white wine before both decided to have the trout amandine.

Later Ashley folded her napkin neatly to tuck it beside her plate. She smiled at Jim.

"Feel better now?" he asked, smiling back. "I do. That was delicious."

"Ummm, yes."

"Dessert?"

"I shouldn't," she murmured, although her eyes faithfully followed the pastry cart a waiter was slowly guiding from table to table. "But that Boston cream pie does look good."

"Then have some," Jim urged. "I will too. After all, we're taking time off to do what we please and relax and enjoy ourselves."

"Yes, but I won't be enjoying next week if I have to live on carrots every day to make up for my calorie intake this weekend."

"I don't think you have any reason to worry about a little splurge," he said, allowing his eyes to travel over her upper body. "You look terrific to—"

"Jim, how you doing?" a booming voice interrupted him at the same time that a heavy hand clapped down hard on his right shoulder. "Son of a gun, I didn't expect to see you here."

Recognizing the voice, Jim rose quickly to shake hands with the bearded man who stood next to his chair. "Great to see you, Pete. How's it going?"

"Same as usual," Pete replied, then clapped Jim's shoulder again. "I saw you sitting over here and just wanted to come tell you I saw you on the Callahan show the other night and agreed with everything you said. These radio psychologists are a menace. Every one of them should be taken off the air." Nodding emphatically, he looked at Ashley and smiled, then returned his attention to Jim. "Come on, don't be selfish. Introduce me to your friend here."

Glancing sideways at Ashley, his expression close to apologetic, Jim complied. "Dr. Ashley Miller, Dr. Peter Simmons. He runs a behavioral clinic in Denver."

Pete Simmons's smile deepened as he inclined his head. "Delighted to meet you, Dr. Miller. Are you a psychiatrist too?"

"No. A psychologist," she answered simply. "I guess you haven't ever tuned in my call-in program on

KTSG. I host one of those radio shows you think are such a menace."

Groaning, Pete stared at Jim. "Well, after I pry my foot out of my mouth, I'll leave you two alone and get back to my own table." He turned to Ashley with a weak smile. "Maybe you'd like to forget we ever met, Dr. Miller."

"Don't tempt me, Dr. Simmons," she replied dryly, her eyes unreadable. "I might take you up on your offer."

"I hope you won't," he said sincerely before shaking Jim's hand again. "See you later. Right now I think I'd better slither into a corner somewhere."

Jim grinned. "Might not be a bad idea." But after Peter Simmons left the table and he settled back down in his chair again, his smile vanished and he surveyed Ashley silently.

She was aware of his penetrating gaze. "Well, you and Dr. Simmons will probably have one fewer radio program to protest in a couple of weeks—mine. When I told Nelson I couldn't do the broadcast tonight, he acted relieved. He didn't even want Dad to fill in for me and finally told me why. Because of Benton Hall's story in the *Record,* Perry Meredith and the other owner of KTSG have decided to pull my program off the air for two or three weeks. And I doubt very much you'll ever have to hear another segment of 'Let's Talk.' This is the beginning of the end."

Jim's jaw tensed. "When did you hear about this?"

"Wednesday night, after I told Nelson I wanted to take tonight off."

"Why didn't you tell me?"

She shrugged. "I guess I just didn't want to think about it this weekend. We're supposed to have a relaxing time."

"But have you really been relaxed since we left Boulder?" he challenged. "I don't think so. You've been unusually quiet, and I'd like to know why you didn't mention what happened."

"I just told you why. I didn't want to talk about it this weekend."

"Especially with me?"

"With anybody."

"Are you sure you're being perfectly honest with yourself?" he questioned, his dark gaze searching, his tone serious. "Maybe you don't want to discuss this with me because you blame me for the station's decision."

"Well, you have to accept some responsibility. After all, you started the controversy in the first place," she answered truthfully but added a resigned smile to her words and shook her head. "But it's not your fault Benton Hall is writing outrageous stories about us that—"

"Stories?" Jim hastily interrupted. "There's been more than one?"

"Oh, yes, there was another one in this morning's *Record.* Polly called this morning before you picked me up and mentioned it when she told me Hall had had the nerve to come by to ask for another interview. I had her read some of it to me—just another piece of fiction held together with a fact or two but mostly skillful insinuation. Maybe he's planning to do a series of exposés on us. Polly got rid of him in a hurry by telling him I was out of town. She didn't tell him where I was, but I wouldn't be too surprised if he tracked us down here."

"I doubt that," Jim said, his voice ice-edged, his jaw tensing. "A newspaper with a small circulation like the *Record* has to operate on a shoestring budget and probably couldn't finance even a trip to Vail."

"Hope you're right. I'd hate to have to try to dodge Hall and a photographer the whole weekend."

"I think I'll have a talk with my lawyer when we get back to Boulder."

"That might be wise." Ashley took a deep breath, then released it in a soft sigh. "Anyway, it's not your fault Hall's made everything more complicated. So no, I don't blame you for Meredith's decision." She grinned. "Sure, you started the whole mess, but I can't blame you for not knowing how it might end up."

"You make that sound like a joke, but people rarely say things they don't mean even if they try to act like they're kidding. Was that a hint of resentment I heard in your voice?"

"No, I don't think so. Look, for a while I did resent what you were doing, but now I accept the fact that we have a difference of opinion and that you don't approve of my radio program."

"Your program doesn't concern me nearly as much as Merv Wheeler's in L.A. and some of the others across the country—the ones hosted by people who are using the media to promote themselves. That's not why you're doing what you do. You try to help your callers with their problems, and though I still have reservations, I imagine you do help some. I realize you truly want to."

"I know that. If I thought you didn't at least respect my position, I wouldn't be here with you right now," she told him, then dismissed the topic with a wave of her hand. "Now, let's drop the subject. We came here for a relaxing weekend and I plan to make the most of it, beginning with some of that Boston cream pie."

Smiling, Jim caught the attention of the waiter attending the pastry cart.

An hour later, after buying a few groceries in town,

they drove back to the house in the pines and unpacked in the single upstairs bedroom, which was actually a loft overlooking the great room below. Energized by the delicious meal, Ashley was ready to hit the slopes but grimaced as she wriggled into her bright red ski suit and raised the zipper of the pants.

"Maybe I should've passed up dessert," she commented. "These things feel more snug on me than they did last year."

"I like well-rounded women," he teased, reaching over to pat her bottom as she slipped into her matching parka.

Saturday it snowed. Light, drifting flakes dusted already powdery ski runs, and around mid-morning Ashley and Jim rode the lift up the mountain. She was a good skier, not a champion but fairly expert, and his skill matched hers. They stayed mainly on the easier advanced runs until after a leisurely lunch in the base lodge. When they walked back outside to retrieve their skis from the racks, the rising wind flung the feathery snow against their faces. One flake caught like a shimmering diadem in the thick upper fringe of her right eyelashes.

With gloved fingers he gently brushed it away, looking down at her, his eyes taking in her features. Healthy color bloomed in her smooth cheeks. Cold tinted the tip of her slightly snubbed nose. He kissed her lightly before they each positioned their leather-lined plastic boots in the step-in toe and heel bindings of their skis, then glided off toward the lift lines together.

Jim motioned her toward the shortest line. "Let's try Prima. How about it?"

"That washboard! Lord, I haven't been down Prima in over two years, and the last time I tried it I thought

I'd kill myself before I ever got to the bottom. But what the heck?" she said laughingly, lifting her ski poles out of the snow, pointing her thumbs toward the gray sky. "It was exciting, so I'm game if you are."

He was, but after they took the lift up and got off at the station ramp closest to the top of the notoriously bumpy run, she wondered if she was being a bit foolhardy. Perhaps she was, but somehow that vague threat of danger exhilarated her. Still, her heart pumped a little faster when they snowplowed to a stop at the verge of the steep slope. She looked down and suppressed a gasp, seeing the impressive moguls, mounds of snow built up by many skiers carving their turns in the same place. The bottom of her stomach did a little downward dip.

"Look at the size of those moguls!" she exclaimed softly. "Some of them are waist-high."

"We can make it. Race you down."

"That's okay. You go first."

"Let's start together."

The instant he pushed off and swept over the sharp edge of the slope, she followed, a competitive spirit reawakening in her. The sheer drop took her breath away for an instant, but she recovered quickly and concentrated all her attention on the snowy course before her. The wind swept through the strands of hair peeking out from beneath her red hood, invigorating her. Jim was only a few feet ahead of her. Wanting to catch up with him so they could reach the bottom of Prima together, she thrust her ski poles down harder and carved her turns around the moguls faster and more sharply until she was even with him. The terrain was too treacherous for her even to risk glancing sideways at him to give a victorious grin. Looking ahead, she tried to plot her downward course but made one minor miscalculation and tried too abrupt a turn to the right. The tip of one ski plowed into a mogul and she went head over heels in the air, bounced against another high mound of snow and finally landed on her back, her breath knocked out as she skidded to a halt, arms outspread, about fifteen feet down the slope.

Unable to move, not wanting even to try, she lay sprawled there, staring at the cloudy sky and the snow that drifted down to land upon her. Luckily her skis had automatically released on impact, so her legs hadn't gotten tangled in them, but that stroke of good fortune didn't cross her mind the few seconds she lay there trying to breathe again. At last she managed a series of quick, shallow gasps. Then Jim snowplowed to a stop beside her. "Are you all right? Feel like anything's broken?"

"When I get over being numb, I'll let you know," she gasped. At last she moved her arms and legs gingerly, then slowly sat up, shaking her head to clear the fuzziness. "I still seem to be in one piece. Do you see my skis? Let's find them so we can finish this roller-coaster ride."

"Sure you feel like skiing down?"

"I have felt better." She groaned, getting to her feet. "I guess I'm just too old for a slope like this."

"You're only as old as you feel."

"Exactly, and right now I feel about two hundred and three."

Smiling, Jim brushed the snow off the back of her parka while she blew a wisp of hair away from her lips and tucked it in under her hood again. Spotting both her skis lying at odd angles behind a mogul to her right, she went to retrieve them, pressing a hand against the small of her back. He frowned.

"Why are you holding your back?" he asked when

she came back and stepped into the heel and toe bindings. "Does it hurt that much?"

"I just felt a little stiff for a second. Nothing serious, although I'll probably be sore tomorrow."

"Maybe we can help that. I'll give you a good back rub when we get back to the house."

"Hmmm, I could use one, after a long hot bath," she said, thrusting the tips of her poles in the snow and doing a couple of quick knee-bends to limber up a little. "Well, we might as well get this over with. Maybe—just maybe—I can get to the bottom without any more spills."

As she pushed off, he followed, and several minutes later they reached the base lodge without further mishap. Deciding to call it quits for the day, they drove to the house, where Ashley made a beeline for the bathroom upstairs, filled the tub with water as hot as she could stand it, and added a generous amount of bubble bath. As she sank into the frothy foam a few moments later, she sighed with pleasure, feeling her entire body immediately begin to relax. Humming, she rested her head back against the tile, occasionally moving her arms and legs to create her own little whirlpool. Quite content, she closed her eyes, enjoying the sensation of silky water on her skin. She dozed for a while, and it was only when Jim knocked once on the bathroom door, then came right in carrying two glasses of white wine with him, that she roused herself.

"Heavens, I'm having my bath, James," she said, pretending to be shocked. "How dare you just come in this way?"

"I didn't hear any movement in here and figured you'd gone to sleep. Thought I'd better wake you up before the water got cold and you caught pneumonia," he replied casually. "And there's no need for you to feel modest. After all, I am a licensed physician. Think of me as a doctor right now instead of a man."

An impossible feat. When he kneeled on the cushioned mat beside the marble tub and handed her a glass of wine, she felt that familiar singing of the senses he always evoked in her by his very nearness. In a cream-color cable-knit sweater that accentuated his sun-browned skin and wide shoulders, and tan cord slacks, he was as attractive as ever. She gave him a soft smile as he touched the rim of his glass to hers with a wry toast.

"To Prima."

"Oh, please, anything but that," she protested, raising her eyes. "I'm never going to let anyone talk me into trying that run again. Let's toast something else."

"How about the future?"

"Great. I'll drink to that," she said, taking a sip, watching as he did too. She swallowed. "Ummm, this is good."

"Yes," he murmured, though his mind wasn't on the wine. Looking at her smooth shoulders, seeing the pale honey tint of her breasts through the veil of iridescent bubbles, he put his glass on the floor. Leaning over the marble edge of the tub, he gently blew at the bubbly drape, needing to expose the rounded flesh of her breasts.

An intense rush of delight careened through her as his warm breath caressed her, and when his hand glided over her, exposing her rosy nipples, she smiled and slipped her wet fingers between his. "Hey, wait a minute, Doctor. You promised me a back rub, but I'm getting amorous advances."

"Right you are. Sorry," he murmured, lazily returning her smile while settling back on his heels. Like a strong spring uncoiling, he rose to his feet, raising his palms. "Okay, get out of there and you'll have your back rub. Bring any skin lotion with you?"

"There on the countertop by the lavatory. The yellow bottle," she said, rising gracefully out of the tub as he turned his back. After drying off, she wrapped herself in a soft apricot towel, then followed him out the door and across the adjoining bedroom. At the bed he threw back the covers, glanced back at her and beckoned her to him, crooking a finger.

"Come on. And take the towel off."

Without hesitation, she did. Exciting warmth spread over the surface of her skin as Jim's eyes drifted over her, but the heated flush subsided when she lowered herself onto the mattress on her stomach and his hands flowed almost impersonally across her shoulders. Fully clothed, he kneeled astride her, poured a dollop of unscented lotion into one cupped palm, rubbed it between his hands, then applied it to her delicately structured back.

Expertly massaged, Ashley relaxed, feeling as if she were sinking into the firm yet yielding mattress beneath her. Her flesh tingled and warmed the very marrow of her bones as Jim's large yet gentle, capable hands roamed all over her, kneading the muscles of her calves and the backs of her thighs, then the arching expanse of her back again and the slope of her shoulders. Soft, contented sighs escaped her parted lips.

The pearl-gray light shining in through the window played over her satin skin, outlining curved contours, fading into shadow along her slim waist. Explosive desire built in Jim, yet he tried to dampen the hot eruption of passionate fire as he continued to run his hands over her slender body. But as she moved languidly beneath his ministering touch, his self-control snapped.

"Ashley," he whispered huskily, turning her over and

parting her long legs. He moved between them, his hands coursing upward, ever upward, along her inner thighs. "I need you."

"Jim," she breathed, throbs of pleasure rippling forth from the center of her being as his fingers drifted over her. Her drowsy blue eyes darkened and held his. "You make me feel so good."

"Baby," he groaned, lowering her hands between them until her fingers feathered over his rigidly aroused masculinity. "I've been wanting us to make love all day."

"Let me undress you," she whispered, slipping his sweater off before her fingers floated down to undo the buckle of his belt.

Sunday morning they skied, but they didn't tackle Prima again. When they returned to the house around eleven, Jim immediately swept Ashley up in his arms and started up the steps.

"We really should start making lunch," she gasped, despite the searing thrill that arrowed through her. "Jim, listen, we—"

"We'll have lunch out."

His warm lips covered hers, and she offered no further protest.

Around five in the afternoon, after tidying the house, they left Vail, heading home to Boulder. The snow had ceased falling; above them stars glittered like diamonds in the clear purple sky. When Jim left the expressway at her exit, then drove on to turn onto her street, Ashley was disappointed. Deep in her heart she had wanted him to ask her to go home with him. He parked at the foot of her driveway, got out to remove her canvas suitcase from his trunk and walked around to her door as she opened it to get out. He escorted her up the steps of the porch and took her house key to unlock the door.

"You were right; I needed some time off," she said quietly, standing on tiptoe to brush a kiss against his right cheek. "Thank you for the weekend. I—enjoyed it."

"So did I."

Nodding, she started across the threshold, but suddenly his hand encircled her upper arm and he turned her back around to face him.

"You must know by now that you mean a lot to me," he said, his deep voice soft as velvet. "I want to live with you. Here at your place or out at mine. Whichever you want, Ashley."

"But, Jim, I—we—oh, God, I don't know what to say," she stammered, totally unprepared for this. "I mean—I—my lord, can you imagine the stories Hall would write if we—we actually lived together? I don't think . . ."

"I don't want an answer now," Jim put in, silencing her with light fingertips against her lips. "Take a few days to think it over. I won't pressure you. I won't come to see you or even call. I won't do anything to influence you. You have to make your own decision."

"But Jim, I—"

"Good night, honey," he whispered, his hand on her elbow impelling her into her living room. Then he pulled the front door shut and walked down the porch steps, thrusting closed fists into his trouser pockets. He wanted to live with her; he needed her close beside him. And he suspected she needed him almost as much. Surely she would say yes to him in a day or two—he hoped.

CHAPTER ELEVEN

Tuesday morning Colette visited Ashley in her office. Cheeks flushed, nervously puffing at her cigarette, she waited while Ashley escorted a patient out the door, then squeezed his hand reassuringly before he left.

"Save some of those soothing words for me, sis. Care to be my shrink today?" Colette wisecracked, walking into the office. Settling on the sofa, she reached for the nearest ashtray. "Or maybe I should just take another tranquilizer."

"Still feeling really down?" Ashley asked sympathetically after closing the door and taking the chair across from her sister. "You seemed to be a little cheerier last week. I thought the group therapy sessions must be helping."

"Oh, I guess they are, and it's not my poor taste in men that's making me crazy today anyhow. I've just been to the dentist," Colette explained, her face pained. "And you know I've always been terrified of dentists."

"Well, that runs in the family. I get the shakes two or three days before routine checkups," Ashley said, then smiled reminiscently. "Remember how we used to get each other in a panic whenever Mom got us appointments with old Dr. Beckman? By the time we got into the chair, we were worked up to a frenzy. Poor man, he never could help us relax no matter how hard he tried. I think he probably dreaded seeing us as much as we dreaded seeing him."

"I doubt that very much," Colette said, tapping the ash from her cigarette. "And getting older isn't helping me any. Nowadays I can get into a panic all by myself. I thought I'd never get to sleep last night; I couldn't stop thinking about this morning."

"What did you have to have done? Anything really painful?"

"He just filled one tiny cavity." Colette shuddered. "But that awful drill . . ."

"I know, I know," Ashley murmured, then brightened. "Maybe we should try hypnotism. It can be very effective sometimes."

"I doubt it would work for me. Where dentists are concerned, I think I'm beyond hope."

"But at least you're feeling better about yourself in general, aren't you?" Ashley inquired gently. "You seem to be. Is the group therapy helping?"

"Yes, I think it is, slowly. It's good to know that other people who are going through divorces feel some of the uncertainties I do. Misery does love company, I guess."

"I wouldn't put it that way. It simply helps to know you're not all alone. So, now that you're feeling better, have you gone out with the physics teacher at your school who's always asking you to?"

"No. And I'm not going to go out with him. I plan to steer clear of all men except Dad for a long time."

"But, Colette, you—"

"I'm going to do what you've done until recently— avoid getting involved with anybody. Maybe in three or four years . . ."

"You don't have to turn into a hermit. Going out

with a man once in a while doesn't mean you have to get involved."

"To you it doesn't, but you know me. I get involved at the drop of a hat," Colette replied, then hastily turned the tables on her younger sister. "Speaking of involvements, how's it going with you and Jim Saxon?"

"He wants us to live together," Ashley blurted, needing to talk and hoping for advice. Since Sunday night, when Jim had made the suggestion, she had thought about him almost constantly. True to his word, he hadn't come to see her or even called, giving her time to think, which she had done until she thought her brain waves might short circuit with the overload. Conflicting emotions yanked her back and forth. The thought of sleeping with him every night and awakening in bed beside him every morning created a joyous thrumming in her heart. Not wanting to get involved with him was no longer a consideration. She was involved and ached to be with him. Yet . . . it wasn't nearly that simple. All these thoughts ran through her head during the few seconds she looked unseeingly at Colette. Finally she flipped her hands, palms up. "What do you think of that?"

"You want the truth?"

"Sure. I wouldn't have asked if I didn't."

"All right, the truth is I think Mom and Dad would have fits if you started living with Jim."

"Oh come on. They'd probably be a little concerned at first, but that wouldn't last. They know life-styles have changed and they're progressive thinkers."

"They're progressive thinkers where other people's daughters are concerned, not their own. Not us, Ashley. They're as human as anyone else, and to them, we're still their little girls. They don't want us doing anything that might seem the least bit improper."

"In a way you're right. But I think they'd eventually understand if I decided to live with Jim. I really do," Ashley said sincerely. "They're not my problem. I can't decide what to say to Jim because of that idiot Benton Hall who's been writing stories about us. I know you don't read such trashy newspapers, but maybe Dad mentioned the articles that have been coming out in the *Record*."

Colette's lips curled. "Yes, and I read a couple of them. Never seen such garbage in my life. Try not to let them bother you."

"But can you imagine what Hall would write if Jim and I *lived* together?" Ashley softly exclaimed. "He's very good at making snide insinuations seem like the gospel, and he'd make us seem like conspirators manufacturing a controversy just to get publicity for 'Let's Talk.' I want to be with Jim, but Hall could really hurt our reputations . . ."

"I'm not so sure of that."

"But what if he can? And what if Jim's interest in me doesn't last? I'll be hurt if we live together awhile, then he just ends it."

"I don't know what to tell you; I wish I did." Colette sighed heavily. "But I've told you I can't give you advice about men." Glancing at her watch, she stood. "Better run. I only took half the day off to go to the dentist. And you probably have another patient waiting to see you." Pausing beside Ashley, she reached down to pat her shoulder. "Sorry I'm not any help."

After Colette left, Ashley decided it hadn't been very fair even to ask for advice. This was a decision she had to make alone. But she was no closer to deciding and glad she'd be greeting her next patient in a minute or two. Concentrating on someone else's problems would temporarily take her mind off her own indecision.

Late that afternoon, while Ashley jotted down her observations about the patient she had last seen, Polly eased open her door, wearing a mysterious grin.

"Something's arrived for you," she announced, her grin widening when she glanced back over her shoulder. "Want me to have it brought in?"

"Sure," Ashley answered, then gasped as a young man appeared in the doorway maneuvering a four-foot-tall stuffed cat into the office. Black and white plush, it sat on its haunches with its tail curled around its front paws, sporting bristly nylon whiskers and shining green eyes. She shook her head unbelievingly. "Good Lord, where in the world did that come from?"

"Here's the note that comes with it," the delivery man said, placing a plain white square envelope in her hand. He produced a receipt book. "Sign here, please."

She did, although she was unable to tear her gaze away from the giant cat. After the man left and Polly followed, closing the door behind her, Ashley opened the envelope and extracted a single folded sheet. Her eyes ran over the neat, flowing script, which read, "Changed my mind. This is meant to influence you to say yes. Saw it in a toy store window and had to buy it. Now you have a kitty Ludlow can't possibly intimidate . . . Jim."

"You crazy lovable man," she whispered, rubbing a hand over the stuffed cat's plush fur and knowing in that moment that she would probably say yes and live with Jim. But before she made a verbal commitment, there was something she had to ask him first. He had said she meant a lot to him; she needed to know exactly how important she was to him.

That evening Ashley drove to Jim's house. The roads were fairly clear of snow except for occasional patches lightly icing spots on bridges and shady curves. She was careful, and even Jim's winding drive gave her little trouble, her wheels only spinning once for a second or so as she went up the gentle rise. Parking in front of the house, she was relieved to find several lights on inside. She hadn't called before driving out. Giving in to strong impulse, she had decided to surprise him.

Smiling to herself as she thought of the huge stuffed cat he had sent her, she got out of the car and walked to the front door, snow crunching beneath her boot heels. Automatically smoothing her hair with one hand, she rang the bell and only had to wait a few moments before Jim answered in his shirt sleeves, his cuffs rolled up to his elbows.

His brows lifted for an instant and he opened the door wider. "Ashley, hello. Come in," he invited, ushering her into the foyer. "Here, I'll take your coat." After doing so and hanging it in the small closet, he directed her into the great room. "Sit down and I'll get you a drink. I've already got one."

"Nothing for me, thanks," she said, making herself comfortable on the sofa. "I just wanted to thank you for James."

Sitting down beside her and picking up his glass, he cocked his head to one side. "James?"

"The stuffed cat you sent me."

"You named him James?"

"Well, it seemed the most appropriate choice, since you gave him to me," she explained wryly. "Guess it's not very original, but I don't have any experience giving names to cats four feet tall."

Tugging at the loosened knot of his tie, Jim nodded. "It is a big cat, isn't it?"

"I'll say. And you made Polly's day by having it delivered to the office. She liked James very much, and I do too. I'm not all that sure Ludlow shares our feelings, though. I took James home before coming here and Ludlow came in for his dinner pit-stop and got to meet the newcomer."

"And what was his reaction?"

"He spat at him," she said, making a funny little face. "Then he streaked like lightning underneath the couch. But finally curiosity got the better of him and he came stalking out, circled around, sniffed James a few times, then curled up between James's paws and took a nap. As if to say, Maybe I can't intimidate this cat but he can't intimidate me either."

Jim's answering smile neatly etched the dimples in his lean cheeks.

"I came over tonight to tell you something else, too," Ashley added as a strange silence seemed to settle between them. "Perry Meredith called me late this afternoon. KTSG has been getting so many calls from listeners upset because 'Let's Talk' hasn't been on for nearly a week that he's decided to put me back on the air tomorrow night. He's not taking Benton Hall's ridiculous stories about us seriously now since none of the reputable newspapers have bothered to pick up on it."

"Good," Jim murmured absently, taking a sip of his drink. "That's good, Ashley."

Disappointed by his lackluster reaction, she thrust her chin out a little. "Well, knowing how you feel about my program, I didn't expect you to stand up and cheer about this, but I did expect you to at least feel a little glad for me. But maybe you're really sorry my program may not be canceled despite all you've said about it not being one of the real targets of your crusade. Is that it?"

"No, it isn't, Ashley," he told her, his tone so sincere she had to believe him. "I *am* glad for you and I didn't mean to sound like I'm not, but . . ."

"Something's wrong," she said softly as the realization suddenly dawned on her. "Something that has nothing to do with my program. What is it, Jim?"

Ice chinked against his glass as he took the last swallow of his drink. He put the cut-glass tumbler down on the table next to him, wearily rubbed the back of his neck and sighed. "The patient I talked to you about—Benjamin, the suicidal young man . . ."

"What?" she prompted gently, although her heart skipped several beats as his voice trailed off. She dreaded hearing what he might be going to say. "Did he . . ."

"He attempted suicide again this afternoon."

"Attempted? Meaning he didn't succeed? He's still alive?"

"Yes, after several transfusions. Damnit, he's extremely intelligent and sly as a fox. Somehow, in the hospital psychiatric ward, he managed to get his hands on a glass, which he broke and . . . a nurse just happened to find him in the bathroom in time." Jim struck his closed fist against his other hand. "If she hadn't gone in when she did, he would have succeeded."

"Oh, Jim," Ashley murmured, feeling guilty for jumping to conclusions before trying to find out why he was in such a troubled mood. Lifting a hand, she touched his jaw. "I'm really sorry he tried again. Maybe it'll be the last time."

"Or maybe it won't. He's more deeply psychotic than I thought, and I should have realized that before today."

Shaking her head, she cupped his face in both hands. "Listen to me. The other night you lectured me about working too hard too long and risking burn-out. Now it's my turn to give you a sermon, one I'm sure you've heard before. But maybe you've forgotten it, because you sound like you're blaming yourself for what Benjamin did this afternoon. You can't do that. You're human, and he hasn't been your patient very long, has he? Probably not nearly long enough for you to really be able to help him. Better than anyone else, you should know that's going to take time."

"If I get that time," Jim uttered.

"I think you will."

"I suppose I think so, too, most of the time. But I went to the hospital this afternoon and saw him . . . Hell, I thought maybe I'd be doing something more constructive if I was on the ranch rounding up cattle instead of trying to deal with mentally disturbed people."

Ashley nodded understandingly. "We all have those kinds of doubts, don't we, at one time or another?"

"I guess we do. And this is one of my times," Jim confessed with an endearingly sheepish smile. "Maybe I just need a little tender loving care."

"Then that's what I'll give you," she murmured huskily, running a hand over his thick, sandy hair when his arms went around her waist and he rested his head in the hollow of her shoulder. She felt he needed her, and the feeling was exquisite. She knew how much she needed him. If he needed her only half as much, she could be content. Love making her heart ache with happiness, she held him, stroking his broad back, touching her lips to his forehead, his temples, his cheeks again and again.

Soothed by her comforting for several minutes but slowly aroused by her very sweetness, he felt the fiery stirring of hot desire erupting inside him. His mouth captured hers as he suddenly straightened and drew her into his cradling arms across his lap. With the tip of his tongue, he tasted her honeyed lips, parted them and tasted the sensitive flesh of her mouth. Her tongue toyed erotically with his, stoking the fire burning in him. Pressing the edge of one thumb into the hollow of her chin, he opened her mouth wider before tenderly catching her soft lower lip between his teeth. The need to possess her totally ran like a river of flame through him.

Ashley clung to him, giving him back kiss for kiss.

Her ardent response drove him wild. The feel of her warm, pliant body pressing against him was more than he could withstand. His hands cupped her breasts, fingers moving with tender aggression over her flesh. He lowered the back zipper of her dress, whispering arousing messages in her ear.

"Kiss me," she whispered back, then uttered a muted protest when he drew away from her instead.

"Come here, baby," he said, lowering himself onto his knees on the thick, soft rug in front of the blazing fire and drawing her down before him, where he swiftly slipped her dress off over her head. In the glow of the flames he trailed feather-light fingertips over her skin along the top of her slip before pushing the straps from her shoulders and down her arms. Nibbling the side of her neck, he undid the back hooks of her bra and cast the lacy garment aside. He straightened, looking at her while he bared her lovely body to the waist, his dark, glinting eyes sweeping over her with passionate intent. "You're so beautiful."

"So are you, and I want to see you," she murmured, on her knees facing him as she took off his tie and shirt. Moving closer, she wound her arms around his neck, her warm breasts straining against the hard, muscular contours of his chest. "Now kiss me."

Their lips met and parted, met and parted again and again. Unconquerable desire quickly consumed them, and soon they were both naked, lying together on the plush rug, touching, caressing, exploring each other with ardent abandon. Ashley moved her hands over him, charting the powerful line of his back to his tapered waist and taut buttocks. His warm breath tickling her skin, he kissed the hard-nubbed peaks of her breasts, her abdomen, her thighs.

"Take me," she breathed, lightly scraping her nails along the backs of his thighs. "Take me now, Jim."

"Yes," he muttered hoarsely, thrusting into her enveloping warmth as she arched upward to receive him.

Tonight she truly felt he needed her, emotionally and physically, as much as she always needed him. That special bond between them seemed stronger than ever, and when they soared together to the spire of ecstasy's sweet completion, happiness spread through her and she softly cried his name.

Breathless, she hugged him close. Contentment warmed every fiber of her being.

"Have you decided?" he asked abruptly, rubbing her back. "I want us to live together, Ashley. Are you going to say yes?"

Leaning back against his encircling arms, she looked up at him. "I have to ask you something before I can decide. Sunday night you told me I mean—a lot to you. How much is a lot, Jim?"

He kissed her forehead. "Very much, honey."

"I *love* you," she said with quiet emotion, shaking her head. "Crazy, isn't it? I didn't want to get involved but I fell in love and . . ."

"I love you too!" he whispered emphatically, a genuine catch in his voice as his eyes held hers captive. "I've been chasing you for weeks. I thought you knew that."

"I didn't . . . until now. I needed to hear the words, I guess."

"Then I'll say them again and again. I love you, Ashley. I love you so much."

"And I love you," she repeated, tears of sheer joy sparkling in her eyes as she kissed his chin and the corners of his mouth and his cheeks. "And if you really love me . . ."

"I do," he murmured, easing one thumb back and forth across her softly shaped lips. "You've been playing hard to get, but I never gave up. Doesn't that prove how I feel?"

"I was just being careful. I didn't deliberately play hard to get. I've wanted you to love me for a long time."

"And now that you know I do, what's your answer?" he asked. "I want us to live together. Do you?"

The sheer magnetism of his eyes holding hers made her breath catch, but she managed a nod and at last answered, "Yes, I want to live with you."

"I'm glad, so glad," he uttered unevenly, then took possession of her parted lips before nuzzling his nose in the hollow beneath her left ear. "Want us to live here or at your place? Not that it really matters to me."

"Here. I'd like to live here with you. The house is so secluded and the woods are so beautiful," she told him, entwining her fingers in the hair brushing his nape. "And besides, I think Ludlow will love it here. Think of all the field mice he'll find to chase, even if he is getting too fat and lazy to have half a chance of catching any. That is, if you don't mind him coming with me."

"Bring James along too," Jim said, tracing a fingertip along the bridge of her nose with a smile before lying back on the rug, one arm beneath his head. He looked up at the ceiling for several seconds, then added, "Hey, what the hell, since we know we want to live together, why don't we just make it legal and get married?"

Ashley feigned a bland expression as she propped

herself on one elbow to lean across him. "Excuse me a minute," she said, reaching for the phone atop the table at the end of the sofa.

"You're calling somebody now?" Jim questioned, catching her hand. "Who?"

"The people who put out the *Guinness Book of World Records*. I'm sure you've just earned yourself a place in the next issue as the man who made the most unromantic proposal of marriage in history."

"Very amusing," he said, closing strong fingers around her wrist to haul her down on him before flipping over to move her beneath him. He cradled her face in both hands. "I was trying to sound nonchalant because I didn't want to scare you into saying no. I know that marriage probably frightens you, since Colette has had two bad experiences."

"But I'm not Colette. And you're nothing like the two men she's been married to," Ashley said softly, linking her fingers over the back of his neck. "I don't think she ever really knew either of them. But I believe I know you. And I want to marry you."

"Before you say yes, let me phrase my proposal more lyrically," he teased. "Ashley, my dear, will you do me the honor of becoming—"

"*Yes,*" she declared eagerly before he could finish, holding him close. "I love you and want to marry you and . . ." She hesitated an instant. "And I want to make sure you don't blame yourself if some of your patients don't respond to therapy and treatment as fast as you want them to—like Benjamin."

"I know you do. That's another reason we have to get married. We understand each other and can help each other keep things in perspective. We both have to deal with patients every day, so we need all the understanding we can get."

Her blue eyes searched the depths of his. "Then you do need me?"

"Yes, because I love you."

"The perfect answer," she whispered. "But are you sure you want to be married to a woman who has a call-in radio program like mine?"

"Make you a deal," he bargained. "I'll stop objecting to all call-in programs and concentrate on getting rid of the ones hosted by psychologists as irresponsible as Merv Wheeler *if* you'll join my crusade to get people like him off the air."

"I'll be glad to."

"Well, then, I think we should get married some time this week, unless you want a big fancy wedding."

"I only want you."

"You know what this means, don't you?" he asked, a faint smile tilting the corners of his mouth. "Since you're going to be one of the family, I can tell you the secret recipe for Saxon's chicken supreme."

She laughed. "Now I know I'm really loved."

"You certainly are," Jim murmured, his hands playing adoringly over her. "And I'm going to show you just how much I love you again right now."

"Yes, show me," Ashley whispered, kissing him. And as they joined together in sweet hot passion once more, they both knew the chase had ended. But the loving had just begun.

Now you can reserve March's Candlelights before they're published!

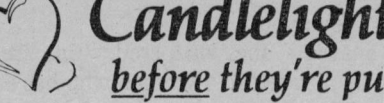

- ♥ You'll have copies set aside for *you* the instant they come off press.
- ♥ You'll save yourself precious shopping time by arranging for *home delivery*.
- ♥ You'll feel proud and efficient about organizing a system that *guarantees* delivery.
- ♥ You'll avoid the disappointment of not finding *every* title you want and need.

ECSTASY SUPREMES $2.50 each

- ☐ 65 **TENDER REFUGE,** Lee Magner 18648-X-35
- ☐ 66 **LOVESTRUCK,** Paula Hamilton 15031-0-10
- ☐ 67 **QUEEN OF HEARTS,** Heather Graham 17165-2-30
- ☐ 68 **A QUESTION OF HONOR,** Alison Tyler 17189-X-32

ECSTASY ROMANCES $1.95 each

- ☐ 314 **STAR-CROSSED,** Sara Jennings 18299-9-11
- ☐ 315 **TWICE THE LOVING,** Megan Lane 19148-3-20
- ☐ 316 **MISTAKEN IMAGE,** Alexis Hill Jordan 15698-X-14
- ☐ 317 **A NOVEL AFFAIR,** Barbara Andrews 16079-0-37
- ☐ 318 **A MATTER OF STYLE,** Alison Tyler....................15305-0-19
- ☐ 319 **MAGIC TOUCH,** Linda Vail....................................15173-2-18
- ☐ 320 **FOREVER AFTER,** Lori Copeland 12681-9-28
- ☐ 321 **GENTLE PROTECTOR,** Linda Randall Wisdom .12831-5-19

At your local bookstore or use this handy coupon for ordering:

DELL READERS SERVICE -Dept. B543A
P.O. BOX 1000, PINE BROOK, N.J. 07058

Please send me the above title(s). I am enclosing $_____$ (please add 75¢ per copy to cover postage and handling). Send check or money order — no cash or CODs. Please allow 3-4 weeks for shipment.
CANADIAN ORDERS: please submit in U.S. dollars.

Ms. Mrs. Mr._____

Address_____

City/State_____ Zip_____

An exceptional, *free* offer awaits readers of Dell's incomparable Candlelight Ecstasy and Supreme Romances.

Subscribe to our all-new CANDLELIGHT NEWSLETTER and you will receive—at absolutely no cost to you—exciting, exclusive information about today's finest romance novels and novelists. You'll be part of a select group to receive sneak previews of upcoming Candlelight Romances, well in advance of publication.

You'll also go behind the scenes to "meet" our Ecstasy and Supreme authors, learning firsthand where they get their ideas and how they made it to the top. News of author appearances and events will be detailed, as well. And contributions from the Candlelight editor will give you the inside scoop on how she makes her decisions about what to publish—and how *you* can try your hand at writing an Ecstasy or Supreme.

You'll find all this and more in Dell's CANDLELIGHT NEWSLETTER. And best of all, *it costs you nothing*. That's right! It's Dell's way of thanking our loyal Candlelight readers and of adding another dimension to your reading enjoyment.

Just fill out the coupon below, return it to us, and look forward to receiving the first of many CANDLELIGHT NEWSLETTERS—overflowing with the kind of excitement that only enhances our romances!

Dell | **DELL READERS SERVICE-Dept. B543B**
P.O. BOX 1000, PINE BROOK, N.J. 07058

Name_____

Address_____

City_____

State_____ Zip_____

Candlelight Ecstasy Romances

- [ ] 290 **BALANCE OF POWER**, Shirley Hart 10382-7-24
- [ ] 291 **BEGINNER'S LUCK**, Alexis Hill Jordan 10416-5-24
- [ ] 292 **LIVE TOGETHER AS STRANGERS**, Megan Lane 14744-1-11
- [ ] 293 **AND ONE MAKES FIVE**, Kit Daley 10197-2-11
- [ ] 294 **RAINBOW'S END**, Lori Copeland 17239-X-16
- [ ] 295 **LOVE'S DAWNING**, Tate McKenna 15020-5-62
- [ ] 296 **SOUTHERN COMFORT**, Carla Neggers 18160-7-17
- [ ] 297 **FORGOTTEN DREAMS**, Eleanor Woods 12653-3-14
- [ ] 298 **MY KIND OF LOVE**, Barbara Andrews 16202-5-29
- [ ] 299 **SHENANDOAH SUMMER**, Samantha Hughes 18045-7-18
- [ ] 300 **STAND STILL THE MOMENT**, Margaret Dobson 18197-6-22
- [ ] 301 **NOT TOO PERFECT**, Candice Adams 16451-6-19
- [ ] 302 **LAUGHTER'S WAY**, Paula Hamilton 14712-3-19
- [ ] 303 **TOMORROW'S PROMISE**, Emily Elliott 18737-0-45
- [ ] 304 **PULLING THE STRINGS**, Alison Tyler 17180-6-23
- [ ] 305 **FIRE AND ICE**, Anna Hudson 12690-8-27

$1.95 each

At your local bookstore or use this handy coupon for ordering:

DELL READERS SERVICE-Dept. B543C
P.O. BOX 1000, PINE BROOK, N.J. 07058

Please send me the above title(s). I am enclosing $_____ (please add 75¢ per copy to cover postage and handling). Send check or money order—no cash or COD's. Please allow 3-4 weeks for shipment. <u>CANADIAN ORDERS</u>: please submit in U.S. dollars.

Ms./Mrs./Mr _____

Address _____

City/State _____ Zip _____